WHY DID THIS HAPPEN TO ME?

John Victor

BALBOA.
PRESS
A DIVISION OF HAY HOUSE

ISBN: 978-1-4525-4092-4 (sc)
ISBN: 978-1-4525-4093-1 (e)
ISBN: 978-1-4525-4094-8 (hc)
Library of Congress Control Number: 2012904447
Balboa Press books may be ordered through booksellers or by contacting:

Balboa Press
A Division of Hay House
1663 Liberty Drive
Bloomington, IN 47403
www.balboapress.com
1-(877) 407-4847

Because of the dynamic nature of the Internet, any web addresses or links contained in this book may have changed since publication and may no longer be valid. The views expressed in this work are solely those of the author and do not necessarily reflect the views of the publisher, and the publisher hereby disclaims any responsibility for them.

The author of this book does not dispense medical advice or prescribe the use of any technique as a form of treatment for physical, emotional, or medical problems without the advice of a physician, either directly or indirectly. The intent of the author is only to offer information of a general nature to help you in your quest for emotional and spiritual well-being. In the event you use any of the information in this book for yourself, which is your constitutional right, the author and the publisher assume no responsibility for your actions.

Any people depicted in stock imagery provided by Thinkstock are models, and such images are being used for illustrative purposes only.
Certain stock imagery © Thinkstock.

Printed in the United States of America

Balboa Press rev. date:3/8/2012

The Beginning

Life is cruel; it's difficult, and it doesn't show mercy. If it wasn't so, how come we were born crying?

It's not the truth because life is beautiful, but it's short, too short to live it in sorrow.

It's normal for those who are happy to see that life is beautiful, but those who are melancholy see it as a bitter life.

The truth says that we may face sad moments, and they maybe much more than moments of joy. It also says that a second of happiness equals many more years compared to sadness.

That second can make us capable of handling the troublesome moments, and it gives us the strength to have patience. That's why it's considered a second source of oxygen after the air that helps us continue in life.

Consequently, how important is that second of happiness to us?

It's far more necessary than anyone can imagine.

When we go through the difficult times; we always resort to others for help, but we are let down when we find out that they don't understand. Our misery increases, and we feel weakness because we conclude we are alone, lost, in this complicated world.

If we claim that others don't understand us, did we ever ask ourselves that we maybe the cause of that? For we may be mistaken in the way we express what we feel inside.

The truth that we believe in is that we are always right, while others are always. Are we really infallible from mistakes?

When we lose hope from the people of our flesh and blood, we wait for the darkness of the night to hide our secrets. Everyone sleeps, except the one who's unhappy, because night is his only companion; it conceals his secrets and reserves the moments of tears and weakness.

It's the full moon night of every month at midnight; we exit with the utmost quietness like thieves, walking further and further from our homes. We get deeper into the forests or the beach sand until we reach a road-block, so we lift our sight a bit higher, and we find that long dark neck, almost in the color of blue, decorated with silver necklace that's similar to a diamond. Around that necklace lay many more jewels covered in gold.

That neck is the sky, and the necklace is the full moon on the fourteenth of that month. Encompassing that necklace are the beautiful night stars, to add the final touches to that painting created by God.

We look left and right and behind us to make sure no one is around. Once we're positive that nobody is there, we begin to cry like children, very quietly so that no one hears us, and we ask:

'Why did this happen to me?'

We know that no one hears us but God, and nature is nothing but a witness to our questions.

Why did this happen to me?

We hear that question a lot, whether it's from those who are close to us, or those who are strangers. We, ourselves, ask that question. That question doesn't refer to a certain group of people because you may hear it from children or even the oldest of age. That question doesn't particulate one incident either because whether it was important or trivial, asking this question is not the inevitable.

Why do we ask that question?
There are many possibilities to answer it; some feel that they don't deserve what happens to them, others feel that it's injustice, you wonder why did it happen to me and not someone else because you believe that they deserve it more than you, but even with all the wonder, it still happens to you and no one else..
Why me? What is the real answer to that question?
The truth is, you won't find a specific answer to that question because to each of us, there is a different answer and analysis. Some people think it's bad luck, as if it's a bad curse that would follow them all their lives; others see it as a consequence for their past mistakes, and what's now happening to them is nothing but punishment; a minority also believe that it's an inheritance, which means you're forced to bear the mistakes of others, like your mother or father, for their past, and you may be the victim, but those are just a small number of people because you need a great amount of courage to admit that you're the real reason for that happening.
But what if the real answer to that question is not any one of those. If you came to a conclusion that we all know the real reason behind all of this, but with our human nature, we always ignore reality. We justify the truth as we wish. This only comes back to mean one thing, and that's running away instead of facing the truth and complete acceptance of what happens without complaining. Although it's not a fact, but surely it's bound to happen, very bound actually.

CHAPTER 1

THE OLD LADY

In this story, there are a few people that wondered; why is this happening to us? Even if they didn't ask the question publicly, they kept asking themselves the same thing. Those people didn't know each other, and they've never even met once before, but one day, a strange thing happened to all of them. What's really strange is that happened to all of them on the same day and the same time. Despite the same thing happening to all of them in different ways, the reason and consequence were the same for all.

Although they didn't know each other, they discovered that something from their past tied them all together, yet they had no idea. Whether they lived that incident or not, it didn't necessarily mean they weren't tied to it in some way.

The people included were eight, four women and four men, but they weren't the same age. Some were old and some were young; the number was more, but death took

1

some of them before they had the chance to know the answer, yet that wasn't a tragedy or a sad thing for them because they will know the answer sooner or later.

Those eight people were:

John, thirty-three years old; he had two daughters, but he didn't have a specific job because he worked at whatever life threw to him.

Martin, twenty-one years of age, was a university student, and he lost his mother at a young age and lived with his father.

Kevin, twenty-five years of age, had a bachelor's degree in law, and he was in a relationship.

Tony, twenty-six years, worked at one of the big company names, and he was also in a relationship.

Madison, twenty-four years, was the lead singer in one of the famous bands.

Jessica, seventeen years, was a student in high school.

Samantha, twenty-two years, worked as a model.

Katherine, twenty-one years, was homeless.

Those are the eight people, but what was that strange thing that happened to all of them?

As for John, he was at the hospital, screaming in his bed, for he suffered from dehydration and severe fatigue, so the doctors made him stay at the hospital. At midnight, John heard a strange noise, almost similar to the sound of a bell that animals wear. He was about to fall asleep when he heard the noise that implanted fear deep within him because it was late at night, and visits weren't allowed, but who would come at that time? What is the story behind that sound?

Darkness hovered over the place, therefore, John couldn't see anything until the curtain on his window opened and let in a considerable amount of light, or at least enough to indicate that his late night visitor was an old woman holding a bell. In spite of the unclear vision at the time, he could make out some facial features; enough for him to figure out that he had never met this woman before. The looks of that old woman weren't hideous, but the incident alone sent chills down his spine.

She was staring at him from the window; full of fear, he asked:

"Who are you?"

With an undecided and trembling voice, she answered:

"That's not important... The important thing is why I came here and what do I want from you..."

" ..So what is it that you want from me?"

"I want you to come with me..."

By now, John was beginning to think that this woman must be insane.

"Where to?"

"To the giant mountains near the volcano."

John laughed mockingly:

"No way... I am sure this is a dream... This isn't happening."

The old lady was beginning to run out of patience by now:

"Do you want me to slap you with this bell to show you that you're not dreaming?"

"Alright... Why do I have to go with you?"

"Don't ask too many questions... You'll find out when you come"

John began to interact more in order to figure out what she wants:

"But I can't even move... How am I supposed to go with you all the way to the mountains?"

"John, don't assume the answer of anything you haven't tried... I must go now; don't be late!"

"How do you know my name, and how did you get in here?"

All these questions were answered by:

"You ask a lot of questions; you'll know everything when you come!"

The curtain closed as the last bit of light left the room, and darkness took over again; John wondered to himself:

"But how am I supposed to leave at such late time?? How am I supposed to go to the giant mountains if they're so far away??"

The voice of the old woman echoed in his ears as she reminded him:

"I told you... Don't assume what you've never tried..."

Kevin was also at the hospital, but he wasn't ill. He suffered from some mental issues. He was tied to a chair to restrain his movements because it could hurt him in the end. The old lady approached him and the ringing of that bell was also present.

Kevin enthusiastically asked:

"Diana?"

The old woman quickly answered:

"No Kevin, I am not Diana."

"Mother?"

She laughed and replied:

"To this extent? You can't distinguish your mother's voice? Kevin, I want you to leave this place and come outside; you have to walk a few steps until you find yourself at the giant mountains.

Darkness was the only thing to be seen, therefore, Kevin's vision was very limited, but he replied, saying:

"Does it seem to you like I can move anywhere?"

She promptly warned:

"Don't assume something you haven't tried; now get up."

She then left, and Kevin began moving his hands, but he couldn't believe he was free. There was nothing tying him down anymore, resultantly, he decided to do what the old woman asked him to do.

As for Tony, he was at his house making coffee late at night because he couldn't go to sleep that night. All of a sudden he heard some strange knocks on the door, and he went to open; he also encountered the old woman, but unlike the others he calmly asked:

"How may I help you?"

"I want you to come with me."

Tony looked at her strangely, and he pushed the door strongly closing it:

"She must be crazy, and I have no time to waste with her."

He quickly went to the kitchen and grabbed his cup of coffee, while he looked outside the window, he was surprised to see the old woman standing there, which made him unintentionally spit his coffee out. She looked very frightening to him from the outside, and he started slowly taking steps backward; he heard the bell sound. To his surprise, she was standing right behind him, which forced him to drop the whole cup in all fearfulness, shattering it to pieces. Then he looked back out the window and saw nothing.

"I am here... Not there," she mocked.

Tony was now trembling in fear:

"Who are you?"

"Come now to the giant mountains near the volcano..."

She then backed out to leave the house, but Tony was still shaking and surprised, and when he finally gained the nerve to ask her some questions, he didn't receive an answer because she had simply disappeared.

Martin was at the hospital with his father, who was suffering from a heart attack, and Martin was standing in the hallway with all the lights on. He was awake with his head leaning on one of the walls, which seemed as if he was trying to take a nap. He suddenly heard the sound of electricity as if it's about to blow, and he looked toward the end of the hallway, only to see that the lights there had gone off and with it came the sound of the bell.

He felt very intimidated because the lights kept going on and off, and it was coming toward him, with the bell sounding every time a light comes on. He looked closely with his legs shaking, and he finally uttered:

"Is there someone out here?"

No one answered, but the lights above him turned off as he heard the voice of that old woman, who told him the same as she had told the others. Martin asked many questions, and as usual, her answers were brief, and she quickly left.

Madison was at a rehabilitation center, and she was asleep when she heard the bell sound and was surprised to see the old woman standing next to her. She told her that she'll be waiting for her at the giant mountains, but before Madison could even react, she disappeared into the darkness.

Jessica was sitting near the pond, where she usually sat, and sometimes she sat there for a very long time, even at night. This time she was also there, she was staring at the water, lost in a whole different world. Her vision was interrupted when she saw the figure of what seemed to be a woman. Jessica didn't know what to do; she didn't know whether it was real, or she was just imagining, until she saw the woman raise her hand whilst holding the same bell. She was still watching all of these events through the water by the reflection of the moon, when she also heard that bell ring. She turned around and saw the old woman, and she told her what she wanted her to do, and despite Jessica's terror, she asked how she would be able to get there without her license, and the old woman told her that she must place both feet in the pond and take one step forward, and that was all she had to do before she departed.

Samantha was at her parents' house; she was in her room, crying badly. She was surprised by a strange darkness when the lights suddenly turned off, but she stopped crying for a second, and yelled for her parents. Instead the old woman answered:

"No... It's me..."

Samantha was immediately terrified. Who was that woman? How did she get here? Why does she ring that bell in her hands? She asked who the old woman was, but the answer was still the same; she told her to go to giant mountains immediately, and all she had to do was to leave the house and take a few steps forward.

Katherine was sleeping in the alley, but she was just the same as every other homeless person around her. She heard the bell ringing above her head, and she woke up, finding the old woman standing in front of her. Katherine wasn't afraid of her. Why wasn't she afraid? Because the looks of that old lady were much better than those are around her, for if a beauty pageant was to take place between those homeless people and that old woman, she would win first place without a doubt. When Katherine looked at her carefully, she begged:

"Would you give me some money miss?"

The old woman smiled and replied:

"I will give you a lot of money, but under one circumstance."

"What's that?" Katherine asked inquisitively.

"That you must come to the giant mountains... Now."

Katherine agreed, but she asked how she was supposed to get there, for the old lady told her what she had told the others; that they must come alone, and she won't be able to lead any of them; she told Katherine to walk only to the end of that alley only, and she vanished.

Everyone, with no exception, couldn't understand what had just happened. It was a very strange and scary situation, but curiosity was the only answer to their questions. If they don't go, they'll never know why it happened to them, or who that woman was. What will happen when they go? What's waiting for them? Those were the questions that haunted each one of them that night.

John got up from his bed, feeling like he'll never be tired again; he was even surprised to find himself at the hospital, and he asked himself what he was doing there, but there was an important matter: to follow the old lady. How is he going to leave at such late time? But he remembered what the old woman told him, and he kept walking. He left his room and didn't find anyone; he kept walking until he arrived at the exit. Throughout his short journey, there were no nurses or even security guards, but as soon as he stepped out of the exit, he found himself at the giant mountains. The same thing happened to Kevin, Martin, Tony, and Samantha; as soon as they stepped out of the hospital or their houses, they found themselves immediately at the mountains. As for Jessica, she did exactly what she was told and placed both feet in the pond, taking only one step forward, while the place transformed to fog right in front of her eyes; it was almost similar to magic. Katherine walked to the end of the alley, and everything around her changed until she found herself at a strange place surrounded by fog.

No matter how afraid you are, be sure that your curiosity is bigger than your fears; this was the fate of everyone, without any exceptions. They don't know what will happen, but with their eagerness, they want to know what is happening to them?

Each one of them thought they were alone, and they never thought they'd find other people who had encountered the same thing. There was one thought they all shared; there is no way that something worse can happen after what they'd already been through. Our question is: what will happen next?

Chapter 2

The gathering

When each of them took their different paths, they found themselves in an unfamiliar place. That place was covered with fog; it was very bad to the point where a person couldn't see their own hand! Everyone stood frozen, for the place sent fear and chills within their souls. The darkness and fog made it impossible to see, and each one of them waited for a signal or order to tell them what to do.

They were right, for all of them heard a noise that sounded familiar to their ears--it was the bell that the old woman was ringing. When they heard that sound, the fog began to ease down and almost disappear; it was vanishing in a quite strange way. It dispersed in front of their sights and formed a very precise road, as if it was telling them to take that path.

Everyone walked along the passage that was formed by fog. They all looked to where a stone building appeared toward the end, which looked like one of the ancient Roman coliseums. The rocks seemed like a circle wrapped around it to form what looked like seats, and in the front was a platform, where the old woman stood and held the bell. That "amphitheater" was very clear to their eyes, but fog surrounded every inch of it, therefore blocking their vision of what lay around the area with the exception of the path that led them there.

When they all arrived, they were surprised to see that they weren't alone. Their eyes looked right and left, as if to ask: Who are these people? What are they doing here?

After they all gathered, the old woman began:

"You may all sit down."

As they took their seats, the roadway they had taken faded, and the fog took its place again around the whole area, making it impossible to see anything besides the inside of that circular coliseum.There, the number seemed to increase by one, a man who was first to open his mouth:

"Hey old woman... What do you want from us??"

She looked back at him and responded:

"You always ask the wrong questions... I won't answer this one right now because I have something to tell all of you, and then you will understand everything. Until then... I don't want to hear a single voice out of you."

It seemed like that man didn't like the answer very much; he stood up and exclaimed angrily:

"You're crazy... I am leaving!!"

She yelled back in a tone the echoed in the ears of those who were present:

"If you cross this circle, you will die!"

The man laughed and didn't seem to care for what she said; as soon as he crossed the circle, he gave out a blood curling scream that sent terror into all of their hearts. That scream indicated that it was the wail of death. The old woman looked at all of them with evil eyes:

"Is there anyone who would like to follow him?"

No one answered, for they were all terrorized by what they'd just seen, but when she heard no response, she continued:

"That's what I thought... Now let's get started... In the center of this circle, an arrow will appear from underground; that arrow will choose a different person each time. The arrow does not choose the same person twice, so there is no need for any of you to change seats. All I want from you is to listen carefully to what I will say when the arrow chooses any of you, and don't rush because you will all know why you're here... Are you all ready?"

Horror and dread hovered among each of them, but their looks indicated that they were ready; they didn't say it though. Suddenly, the arrow came from underground, but it was secured with the roots of the tree. Of course, it caused a small earthquake until it stopped. Its tip pointed towards the old woman, and none of them could comprehend what had just happened. She looked at all of them and ordered to the arrow:

"Turn!"

The arrow turned around as if someone was forcing it to do so, although no one was. It kept spinning until it began slowing down bit by bit. Everyone was thinking of the moment it turns to them; their heartbeats could almost be heard; they were strongly beating as the arrow came closer to one of them. There was no room for anyone to think because in the end, all of them will know what is going on. It finally stopped spinning and chose Tony as the first to go.

CHAPTER 3

TONY

Silence took over that place when the arrow stopped, and they began to look around to see who had been chosen. Everyone was looking at the man where the arrow had stopped; then they directed their eyes toward the old lady, who was looking down. She didn't see the movement of the arrow because all that time she was staring at the ground. When the arrow stopped, she lifted up her head and began looking at all of them:

"When the arrow chooses one of you, I will tell you the story of the chosen one, for his story is what brought him here, and it will be the same for all of you."

She looked at that man and began:

"Tony a twenty-six years of age, and he has a bachelor's degree in accounting. He works at a very high-profile company and earns a great amount of money. He is an example of a serious and hard worker, for that reason, it is difficult for him not to stand out and turn all eyes to him. Since his arrival at the company his touches were very visible.

His life was perfect, but it lacked one element. That element for Tony was like seasoning for food, for no matter how appealing the food may be, it won't have a great taste without seasoning. For him, that seasoning was a woman-- the woman who will share this outstanding life with him.

The good news is that fate still smiled for Tony. One day upon his exit from his workplace, he was walking backwards because he was talking to one of his colleagues, and when he finished, he turned around to walk the right way, but as soon as he turned around, he ran into a young lady. All of the papers in the girl's hands came flying everywhere. Tony was supposed to help her clean the mess up, for he was the one who caused it, but he stood still and all he did at that moment was stare at her.

That look was a look of admiration because the girl was very beautiful. He was still looking at her as she picked up her papers, and she didn't even ask him for help. As soon as she finished picking up all the papers, she immediately got up and asked:

"Do you happen to know where Mr. Toni's office is?"

On that note, Tony scratched his head in embarrassment:

"I am afraid that's me you're looking for..."

But the girl was very serious, and it seemed that she didn't have a definition for joking in her dictionary; she answered in a serious tone:

"I am Kate... The new employee."

"Kate? Ahh Yes. The manager has told me to train you and show you what you're supposed to do. Alright, so follow me!"

Tony led her to her new office and explained that nature of the work she will be expected to do, but he soon remembered how rude he was for not apologizing; he looked at her and said:

"May I take you out for a cup of coffee? You know as some kind of an apology for what happened."

Without looking at him and with no hesitation, she answered:

"No."

"There is a place here that makes amazing coffee;" he stopped for a moment and continued: "My apologies."

She replied with an even more angry tone:

"No!"

Tony was kind of embarrassed for the rejection, but he wanted to shake that feeling off, so he yelled angrily:

"You're a bad employee!" He looked down at his watch and went on: "You're half an hour late for your appointment!"

Kate looked at him and began laughing hysterically because she noticed the redness that was forming on his face. Tony's reply to this was:

"Well it's good that you've finally realized it takes less muscle usage to laugh than to frown!" He headed for the door to exit before she spoke:

"May I invite you for a cup of coffee? You know... Because I was late."

Without even bothering to look at her, he quickly said:

"Of course not!" Although, he did smile while saying so. He turned around to look at her again:

"You look like an angel when you laugh," he left the office.

Even though they started out badly, the admiration was still present. Their looks at each other when they work together were very obvious to everyone who saw them. Finally, they were able to go to that coffee shop and get have their coffee.

The relationship began to take new levels very quickly. One day, they were together, and Kate saw an old couple; she couldn't look away, and Tony quickly took notice.

"I promise you that we will be like them. Even when I see all of your teeth fall out, you will still be the most beautiful girl I've ever seen, and the one I love the most."

The two of them were deeply in love, and no one could remember a day when they'd fought after the night of their first encounter.

All of this giving and harmony meant that their relationship will eventually end in marriage, and that's exactly what happened when Tony and Kate set a date for their wedding. The final date was only one month after their decision, but their planning never took place. A week before their wedding, Kate called Tony telling him to cancel the wedding, and that she didn't want to get married.

It was natural for something like that to cause a shock for Tony, so he decided to go to her, lightning speed, in order to find out what happened, and what was the reason that caused her to call everything off. On the way, Tony's bigger fear was the tone of her voice when she asked him to cancel their plans. He arrived at her house and began calling her name; she answered in a low and melancholy voice:

"I am here..."

He promptly headed toward the source of her voice, only to find piles of napkins laying on the table in front of her; each of these was filled with her tears. Worry struck his heart instantly, for he knew something had happened. He gently walked towards Kate and sat close to her:

"Honey, what happened?" Instead, he was surprised to see her move away. Doubt was filling his heart even though was more sure than anything that he hasn't done anything to deserve all of this. After a long silence, she finally said:

"I am sorry... We have to cancel the wedding!"

Tony smiled strangely in disbelief and replied:

"This is a joke! You want to cancel the wedding just like that, and for no reason?"

She instantly retorted:
"Do I look like I am joking?!"
"But..."
Before he could finish, she interrupted him by yelling:
"Leave me alone!"
Ignoring her request, Tony angrily answered:
"It's not a game, and it's not your decision only to ask for such thing and for no apparent reason!"
With an immediate explosion of tears, she cried:
"That wedding will be cancelled whether you like it or not; it's not up to me or you!"
She got up to leave, but Tony grabbed her wrist tightly, forcing her to look at him. Kate couldn't do anything but throw herself into his arms while still crying. He tried to calm her down and asked her what was going on; Kate's answer was:
"I am scared... I am going to die... I am going to die!!"
These words became another shock to Tony, for he couldn't comprehend or understand them:
"Wait... What do you mean you're going to die?"
Kate was still crying when she finally said:
"I have cancer, and it's at its worst stages... I won't live much longer, and I don't have the same value. Go live your life with another woman!"
Despite the fact that these words would cause a surprise, Tony's reaction was a bit strange; he slapped her at once and said:
"You better not say those words again! No one is going to die here; I love you, and you're going to get better! That's all I know." He looked at her eyes, which contained a tragic message that he couldn't understand; using the same tone she had when she called him, she said:
"Is that what you really want, Tony?"
Without uncertainty, he answered:

"Have you gone mad? Of course that's what I want; I can't even begin to imagine my life without you. You must know that, Kate."

She smiled sorrowly as if she had accepted what he said. He then took her to the hospital, and they went to a specialist for her case. They sat with the doctor in his office, and Tony told the doctor that Kate wants to begin her treatment; the doctor looked at her and asked:

"Do you really want that Kate?"

Kate was staring at the floor in silence; the truth is, Kate didn't want treatment, but Tony interrupted him:

"Yes... She wants to start the treatment."

The doctor looked at him:

"Sir, I didn't ask you... I asked Kate." He looked back at her, but she was looking into Tony's eyes, which looked as if he was begging her to agree, and she didn't want to hurt him, so she answered quietly:

"Yes, I want the treatment."

The doctor then asked her to go to the room next door and leave them two alone to talk, until he comes to her. Kate went to that room, and the doctor and Tony stayed back. The doctor began:

"Do you know that the chance of success for this treatment doesn't even reach 1%?"

Tony looked at him:

"No, and it's not important. All I want is for Kate to recover."

The doctor got up from behind his office:

"Do you know, Mr. Tony, what a woman loves the most?" Tony replied negatively, and the doctor went on:

"That she looks beautiful always, and she turns all eyes to her. What I mean is that when Kate starts treatment, all of her hair will begin to fall down, and she'll become bald and begin to lose her beauty. Do you know what that can lead to? It can lead to suicide and inwardness, but above all of this, it's not worth the trouble and suffering."

Tony couldn't believe what he was hearing and became angry:

"I think that's none of your business. All you have to do is perform your job, and that's it."

The doctor looked at him in pity; of course what he had just said was right, but the doctor had a completely different view; he finished:

"But that's called selfishness from you, Mr. Tony." He then left to check how Kate was doing.

Kate began the therapy, and her hair began to fall down until she became bald. She hid it underneath a wig though, and she created her own world. She never went out because was was embarrassed by the way she looked. Her world was now her room and her sleep only. No friends, no going out, and no connection with the outer world. In contempt of Tony's efforts to help her out, nothing seemed to work, for since she began the treatment, the bright smile she used to have left her pale face; she never smiled.

One day, Tony arrived at the house as usual, and he called for Kate, but she didn't answer. He began searching for her around the house until he found her laying in the bathroom floor, motionless. He quickly called the ambulance, which carried her to the hospital. There, the doctor told him that the reason behind her illness was that she didn't take her medication, and she didn't eat for days. He then proceeded to tell him that she is under God's hands now, for that was the fall that Kate will never be able to recover from."

CHAPTER 4

MADISON

Everyone's attention was directed to the old woman, and their sights were directed at Tony. The good thing was that the situation wasn't as bad as they had all thought when the arrow chooses one of them. Listening to Tony's story proved to them something very important; that they may find the answer to what they've been asking for years... Why is this happening to me?

The old woman looked to the arrow again, and ordered: "Spin!" It began spinning one more and stopped at Madison. The old woman began talking:

"Madison... Doesn't seem as if I need to introduce her to you because she is famous and well-known by all, and I saw your looks towards her when you first saw her. What you know about Madison is what the media carries only, as if the media is something sacred, and anything from it can be taken even if it was lies."

She then continued:

"Madison is a twenty-eight year old who has a bachelor's degree in music. She was in love with music and poetry. Most of you know that most of her band's songs are written and composed by her. She met the members of her band in college because they all had the same interest. When she decided to form the band, there were three members, with her included, it would be four. They all had one dream-- success, and they wanted to take the throne at the list of the "Best Ten Bands in the World". That was exactly what they went after.

One day, and before the band became famous, or before they had even published any song, a girl named Marshall; you know her of course; she is the violin player in the band. She proposed to the band the idea that she wanted to join, but all of the members rejected her offer, excluding Madison.

The reason behind the rejection of this band, which was composed of three girls, not counting Madison, was that the girl named Marshall was a bad example, and she didn't deserve to join. That example was not based on personal level, but on behavior. She was full of hatred, and she never entered something without destroying it. Madison didn't pay much attention to all of these factors because Marshall played the violin very well, and her joining the band would add more to the band without a doubt. As for her behavior, Madison always said that it's personal freedom, so she began persuading the girls based on her own view until they were all convinced about what the leader, Madison, had to say.

Madison was definitely not wrong with her decision because Marshall's addition gave them balance, especially with the fact that they lacked a person who played the violin as wonderfully as Marshall.

The band used to meet in a place near the end of the forest; the area overlooked a large valley, and the sun was very close; it almost gave a feeling that if you reach out, you can actually touch it. That scenery was truly beautiful, and it had the capability to let out a wonderful energy from anyone who visits. For that reason, this was the band's secret spot or the most important place for them, so to speak. All of their meetings were held there.

One day, Marshall came to their place with a huge smile drawn on her face. They all questioned the reason of her happiness, and she informed them that she knows a person who will organize a meeting for them with a famous producer. Their laughs filled the air after the news, and each one of them jumped excitedly, for their dream was only steps away from coming true.

Seems like Madison wasn't wrong when she decided to let Marshall Join; that's what all the members thought. The news for them was a huge push, and the girls began working on the songs they would perform for the producer. They worked on that night and day at the place they counted as their inspiration, and they didn't care for the scary darkness that arrives at night; all they would do is park their cars near the valley and begin working.

The day of the meeting, which was set by Marshall's friend with the producer, finally came, and the girls went to the producer's house. Honestly, it was a mansion, not a house.

They entered despite the nervousness they were having, but it was their chance, and they had to have confidence in themselves because if they didn't, no one else would believe in them either.

The servant led them to a huge garden with a swimming pool that surpassed amazement. Everything was prepared for their visit: the tables, chairs and drinks. Each of the girls brought her instrument; Madison with a guitar, Marshall with the violin, and the rest with the organ and other instruments.

The producer arrived, and he was in his fifties; he was a very kind man as he said to the girls:

"Are you ready?"

At once, they all replied:

"Yes!"

"Then show me what you've got! I am all ears," he continued.

They began playing their music, until Madison began. You all know she has a wonderful voice that delights the ears. She sang one of the songs she had written. Madison's voice wasn't the only outstanding thing, but also her feeling while she closed her eyes; it was enough to take you to another world. Although, she, herself, went to another world while singing because of her integration and amazing feeling.

As for the producer, he couldn't believe what he was hearing; be sure that he went to the world where Madison was and lived it. He was very pleased with what she gave to the point that when one of his servants came to notify him of an important call, he signaled with his hands that he'll answer later.

You can imagine how pleased he was with what he was hearing by how he disregarded the call, and he settled for a signal only. Madison finished, and he wished that she hadn't; he stood up like a child and warmly applauded:

"This is unbelievable! I'd never heard anything like this in many years. What's your name young lady?" Even though he wasn't that old, he was very respectful.

She happily answered:

"Madison."

"Oh my goodness! You're a beautiful young lady, you have an amazing voice, and the song was very outstanding; I'd be an idiot not to accept this gift!"

These words meant only one thing-- their dream had come true. Their reaction was naturally to scream from the amount of happiness, and they exchanged hugs, but the atmosphere didn't lack tears of joy either.

The band's first record was published immediately after that meeting. Now there is nothing to do but reap what they had planted--success. The girls met at their usual place, until Marshall told them that their song will be played on air, and they would enter the competition for the five best songs. The windows and doors in the car were wide open, and the volume as loud as it can go; they had it set on the station that was supposed to play their song, and finally, what they've all been waiting for happened-- their song was played. It's something very hard to describe their joy, but keep in mind that if you ask any singer in the world, what is the best moment of their life, the answer, without a doubt, would be when they hear themselves on the radio for the first time.

That band achieved world-wide fame because everyone has heard of the band "American Girl"; they were everyone's trending topic, and their songs never stopped playing on the radio, or even the small screen. Until now, everything seems to be going just fine, but Madison began feeling something that everyone feels--depression. It's known that depression is caused by one thing, and that's loss of freedom. That's the price of fame; therefore, you can see how their houses are like ravishing paradise; did you ask yourself why they do that? Because these houses are their world and those are the only shelter they have, for they can live in it normally and with freedom.

I can say that what Madison felt was what every famous person feels; it's the feeling of a bird who finds everything it needs and does whatever it wants under one circumstance: to stay within a cage and be deprived of its liberty.

Does fame really deserve that price?

Yes she feels very happy with all the fame and fans, and she can now achieve whatever she wants, but that life was getting filled with depression and boredom. There had to be some way she can let everything out to someone close to her and tell them what she feels. That person was Marshall, the co-leader of the band; Madison began complaining about her psychological state to Marshall. She even told her that she is not eating because of this. Madison didn't know that she was digging her own grave because Marshall's jealousy blinded her. She believes that she was the true reason behind the band's success, but the lights and the media shone on Madison only, disregarding what Marshall had done for the sake of reaching fame. That antagonism filled her heart because Madison never appreciated Marshall's efforts, nor did she deny her hard work, but she just hasn't had a real chance to express those things. Marshall, though, understood it as being clearly overlooked and ignored.

Seems like fate smiled for Marshall to seek revenge, for that was a chance handed to her on a golden plate, and she can't let a chance like that pass. She began telling Madison that she suffered the same thing, but when she turned to drugs, those feelings vanished completely. The truth is that Marshall was a liar because she wasn't a drug-addict, but she said so to encourage her, and to make her obey her orders. Madison completely rejected the idea, but Marshall never lost hope; she kept repeating the same thing over and over.

Madison's doubt, her trust towards Marshall, and her psychological state all lead to surrender and entrance to the world of drugs. She began the feeling of fake happiness, and what Marshall told her was right. She didn't care for anything but drugs and the disguised happiness.

Marshall was like a skilled fisher, who had an experience with bait. She looked in hopes attacking the fish, and that fish was Madison. She had gotten what she wanted, for

Madison swallowed the bait, but a smart fisher not only lets the fish swallow the bait, but he longs for catching that fish and taking it out of the water. So how did Marshall take that fish out of the water?

Things weren't that easy though; Marshall waited almost a year until Madison couldn't leave the drugs; not only that, but she also started buying them in large amounts and storing them at her house to save time. That way she'll have the drugs whenever she needs them, not having to wait every time either.

That was the best chance to strongly pull the bait, because the fish has weakened, and it's much easier to take it out. Marshall notified the police about the large amounts of drugs that Madison kept at her house. The anti-drug authorities raided her house and found very large amounts of illegal drugs, and they arrested Madison and charged her with unauthorized possession of illegal drugs; she was trialed and put into prison for five years.

Let's get back to the fisher; that fisher didn't just take the fish out, for he is hungry, and he must eat to satisfy his hunger. Marshall started a media war that led to a complete destruction of Madison; with money and knowledge of certain people, you can buy the media. The media had nothing else to talk about but Madison, as if she was the first famous person to get addicted; not only that, but one newspaper even wrote a huge headline: "Drug Dealing Madison"

Those newspapers were filled with lies. It was like this: the journalist is presented with a large sum of money, a white sheet of paper, and a pen; then he is told to write anything he can think of about Madison; write and lie; I want Madison to be a page in history. Of course, you may know who wrote about her by reading the newspapers; here are some other headlines of what was said about her:

"Madison is nothing but a Lesbian!"

"Wait! Madison Runs a Brothel!"

"Madison Spits in a Black Guy's Face!"

There are many more, but I will stop at these headlines, which Madison didn't do any of; the only mistake she made was becoming addicted to drugs.

Yes Madison was done; the one that everyone loved and they loved her singing. That beautiful and attractive girl is nothing but an overly skinny girl that you can almost see the shaping of her bones from under her skin, and the darkness under her eyes; she now resembled a ghost.

She left prison after her five year was over, and she was admitted into a rehabilitation center for drug addiction. Prison was a bitter lesson for her because everyone left her, and no one visited her, not even the band members. She was considered dead to them, but she was now at the rehabilitation center.

Do you know that Madison didn't sleep all of these years during her time in prison? Those voices were chasing her; she would cry and hide her face under the pillow to block out these voices. Do you know what those voices were?

They were the voices of her fans; the fans who shouted her name each time she took the stage; the posters they held with her pictures, the symbols and words that were written; "You're America's Queen!" All of that was gone all of a sudden; it's a very difficult thing.

All of you know that the band, "American Girl", broke up and became a thing of the past. Marshall had a good voice, so she became a singer herself. As for the rest, some joined other bands, and others retired from show business."

The old woman once again finished and went on:

"Turn!"

This time the arrow chose Katherine.

CHAPTER 5

KATHERINE

"Katherine, twenty-one years of age; don't let her current look fool you because the truth is: at one point, she had what every other girl dreamt of having. She used to count as one of finest at her university, undisputedly, in her elegance that is. You can smell her fragrant perfume almost from miles away; when Katherine walked in the hallways, all the heads turned toward her and never stopped staring. Yes she is not extremely beautiful, but she has something that attracted you to her; safe to say, she was every guy's dream girl.

Katherine lived her life within a very wealthy family; she lived with her mother and grandmother, but she lost her father a couple of months before her birth. She was a very spoiled child to her mother and grandmother, despite her grandmother having other grandchildren, she had a more special bond with Katherine; the same went for her mother as well. That attitude always caused problems with Jacqueline's, Katherine's mom, brother because he accused

31

his mother of being unfair towards his kids and Jacqueline's daughter. Although, his mother justified it as a matter of Jacqueline and Katherine lived with her, unlike him, who left soon after he got married. He only visited his mother every once in a while.

Jacqueline was twenty-four years of age, and she was a very beautiful woman, but she never got married again, nor formed a relationship; instead, she devoted all of her time to Katherine; she loved her more than anything in this world.

One day when she turned four years old, which was a day that still resides in Katherine's memory, when she turned four years old because that was the day Jacqueline wanted to go out, but Katherine approached her and asked her to take her to the Candy World.

Candy world is one of the finest and most popular candy stores in the country; it was a trade mark in the candy world; you can just spare the words by calling it the candy paradise.

Jacqueline and her mother broke out in laughter; why? Because Jacqueline was the one who planted the love of candy in her daughter; she was very skilled in making any kind of sweets, and she always took Katherine there, to Candy World. Katherine also always helped her mother get the ingredients for the great dishes she made. Will she become a small version of Jacqueline?

Jacqueline told her that she had to go somewhere, and when she comes back, she'll take her there, and she asked her to wait. Jacqueline then left, and Katherine insisted that she wanted to wait for her outside until she came back.

Katherine, that little girl, didn't know that the waiting would never end because that was the last night she would see her mother and talk to her; Jacqueline's tire exploded on the way, and she lost control of the wheel, leading the car to fall into the valley, and Jacqueline lost her life.

Katherine was still waiting, but her grandmother found out; she had to gather the strength to tell her the news. The grandmother was in a very bad situation; how can she tell a little girl such news? How can the little girl understand what death means? It's something way beyond her understanding, but the grandmother, with her years of experience, explained the news using trickery and a simple way that her brain could understand. She told her that her mother will never come back because God called her to him, and that God will call everyone at some point. Without knowing, Katherine began asking when God will call her because she wanted to go to the Candy World with her mother. Her grandmother's eyes filled with tears, for she had to agree with the little girl; she hugged her in tears:

"It's not important when that day will be, but the important thing is that we'll meet in the end; as for Candy World, I will be the one that takes you there someday if you'd like."

After Jacqueline's death, her grandmother did something very strange, and she never explained it. She completely cut off any form of communication or connection between her son's family and Katherine; she sent her to a private school away from her uncle and his kids, and she forbade her to see them. Even when her uncle visited them, her grandmother would send her out so that she won't see them at all, despite Katherine's questions about them. It's something very strange because that was her son, and the kids were her grandchildren. She never answered Katherine's questions, and she ordered her not to ask about them again.

With the exception of that situation, Katherine was blessed with a wonderful life; everything she asked for was given to her, and her grandmother was always with her and took her out everywhere. Not only that, but she encouraged the spirit of cooking that Jacqueline had planted into her; she bought her books and CD's about everything that had to do with sweets. That was what pleased Katherine the most.

When Katherine turned seventeen; her grandmother asked to meet her because she wanted to tell her something important. Katherine came and sat by her grandmother, asking what the important thing she wanted to say was; her grandmother began:

"You're now a young adult, and at this age, you should be very understanding and open-minded. You already know that after your mother's death, I didn't allow you to see my son or his kids. That was something very difficult for you, and I am sure that the same question still resides in your mind. Now is the time for you to know everything; Jacqueline never married in her lifetime, but she had a special love for kids, and she adored them very much. One day she came to me saying that she wanted some money to build a care center for kids. The goal was to paint a smile on every child's face that had lost a father, or those who suffer from illnesses. I didn't stop her, and she went on to build that center, but I didn't see her much afterwards. She would stay there all the time, but I knew that she was safe, and that she was in the best conditions. That world was everything she loved and asked for. One day Jacqueline came to me for the first time with an indescribable psychological state. I asked her what was wrong, and she said that she had found a girl that was barely five months old; for me, it wasn't that big of a deal because Jacqueline was used to this sort of things, but she told me that it was the first time she had felt something different. She had a very hard time explaining that feeling of when she picked up that girl and hugged her. Do you know what that feeling was Katherine? It was the feeling of motherhood, and I told her that. She told me that she wasn't the mother of that child, and I mentioned to her that you don't have to be a mother to have those feelings, but those feelings are a gift from God, and it may be a sign.

The days passed, and she would always come to me and tell me what that little girl did. Everything she said was about that girl. Three months later, I was surprised when Jacqueline came in holding a baby girl. A smile was drawn on her face; she was very beautiful. I asked her who that child was; she smiled and kissed her lightly:

"This is Katherine... My daughter."

You were Jacqueline's daughter, Katherine; the girl she never had, but the one whom she always loved. Things may be clear to you now; I forbade you to see them because they would hurt you with their words, and you were young; you wouldn't understand. They knew you weren't Jacqueline's daughter. I am telling you the truth now, and I know that it's very painful for you. I wanted you to hear this from me and not someone else, so that I won't be a liar in your eyes. What I want from you my darling is to know that you are Jacqueline's daughter despite everything, and you are my granddaughter also. God took Jacqueline away from me, but he replaced her with you. I see Jacqueline in you; your laugh, the way you talk, the way you dress; Jacqueline lives in you."

She finished as she buried her head in her hands and cried loudly. There is no telling what Katherine would do in this case, but it seems like her grandmother was not wrong when she said that Katherine is now an understanding young lady, for she looked at things positively. Yes she is an orphan, but in the place of that she gained a family that consisted of a mother and grandmother. That family made up for everything, and she lived what every girl wishes for. All she could do at that moment was to throw herself into her grandmother's arms, and between the tears of the both of them, Katherine repeated:

"I love you grandmother... I love you."

Katherine continued living her life normally, and the truth was not an obstacle for her. Instead, that was the thing that made her love the family even more. When she turned twenty-one; her grandmother couldn't leave the bed due to an illness. Katherine became like a nurse to her, and she didn't go anywhere else but the university. All of her time was spent by sitting with her grandmother and taking care of her. It was the inevitable that she would have to face the others, her uncle and his kids. Yes she heard all of their hurtful words that reminded her of who she was, and that she was only an orphan. They also accused her of being a gold digger, and that she only plays the role of an innocent girl who loves her grandmother. All of these things deeply saddened her, but she had to endure and be patient just for the sake of her grandmother. She didn't want to worry her with what went on because her illness alone could end her life, so how can she tell her all of these things also?

The illness wasn't the only thing troubling the grandmother, but there was something else that she would always tell Katherine about. She also referred to how hurtful it was to not have her son and his family by her side. She told her that since his marriage, he ignored them and never asked about them until holidays came by. She said that Jacqueline was the only one taking care of her. Katherine could see that he only visited once or twice a week despite her illness, but her grandmother also told her that having her close by takes the place of everything else, and that she never regrets choosing Katherine over them because she was sure that Katherine would be closer and kinder to her than her own son.

The wall of protection for Katherine had fallen, and Katherine felt for the first time in her life what fear meant, or what feeling unsafe really meant. That wall was her grandmother for she had died after her battle with the illness, leaving Katherine alone. Behind that wall are hungry coyotes, whom shining teeth can be seen to inform you that they're thirsty for blood, and if you knew that in front of them was a wounded fawn who can't move; what can possibly happen?!

She knew that she had to leave before getting thrown out, for she didn't belong at that house since the beginning. Katherine left that house after living as a princess in it for many long years--humiliated. She left to start a life that was supposed to be her real beginning-- the life of an orphan. The displacement in the streets without a home, and her only companions would be sorrow and fear. She left the university even though it was her last year, and the sidewalks became her bed. The hard rock's took the place of her soft pillow, and the clothes that people threw out were her blankets."

She finished as the arrow spun again and chose Martin this time.

CHAPTER 6

MARTIN

"Martin, of twenty-one years old, lost his mother at a younger age. His mother didn't suffer from any sicknesses, but she went to sleep one day and never woke up. He lived with his dad without a mother. When he lost his mother, Martin was six years old. He had a weak vision, so he had to wear eye glasses, which had the big lenses. You can imagine what he must have looked like to others; people looked to him as a fool because of those awkward glasses. Also because he was socially awkward, and he never talked, and because of his looks, which caused laughter.

All of these factors led Martin to fall down to the bottom of the "unintelligent students" list in his school at an older age.

As for Martin's father, he loved his wife very much, and losing her left a very sad impact in his heart. Some people have different reactions than others. His reaction was not the best, for he weakened and entered the world of alcohol until he became addicted. Martin always saw alcohol bottles glued to his father's hands.

The wrong decision that Martin's dad made and the loss of his wife reflected one thing: he abused Martin daily, whether it was for a reason or not. His father would let his anger out on him, and he became the victim of anything that happened at the house.

After two years marked his mother's death, Martin didn't know his father was preparing a surprise for him; he didn't even tell him about the surprise, nor did he prepare him mentally for it. Martin was shocked when his dad came in one day with a strange woman; he told him that this was his wife and his new mom. Martin's reaction was very spontaneous when he yelled:

"I only have one mother, and she is with God!"

He then headed to his room with eyes full of tears; his reaction angered his dad, and he quickly pulled his belt out and ran after him. He began beating Martin monstrously, and all Martin could do was screaming in pain. His voice could send chills down anyone's body. Yes it wasn't the first time he had been abused, but that doesn't mean that it wasn't painful. It's also not easy having another woman take the place of your mother.

The oddest thing of what happened thought was that the new wife didn't even move. It seemed as if she was okay with it, for that, Martin's judgment was not wrong. The angels' mask she was wearing hid nothing but a poisonous snake.

Wretchedness took over Martin's life from here, but that doesn't mean he had lived better days in the past; things have just started to get worse than before. It's easy to count everything, but it's very hard to count how many times Martin gets beaten each day. His step-mother abused him every day for no reason; not only that, but she would wait for his dad and spew venom in his brains, making him go mad and continue what she had begun.

That woman had one goal that she longed to accomplish, and that's to force Martin to run away. She didn't want him at the house, therefore, you can justify why she treated him horribly. Although, Martin was strong, and he never lost patience or hope. Despite his father's faults, he still listened to what his wife ordered, but he rejected the idea of sending his son to a boarding school, which she always encouraged him to do. He also didn't agree with the idea of forcing Martin to stay him without continuing his education.

Martin's conditions weren't better outside the home boundaries either, because like I said, he's considered one of the stupidest kids at his school. If you were to ask him how many trash cans are at the school, and where they're place, be sure he will answer that question quite fast.. Why?

Because he was thrown in them by his school mates before, and as soon as they do so, you can hear their laughs disappearing into thin air at the end of each hallway. Martin was hated by everyone, and he never told the teachers of what he encounters, fearing his step-mother. Even though the bruises on his face always opened up opportunities for questions from his teachers, whether they were from his school mates or his parents, but he always justifies them as falling down or other excuses. Martin endured all of these humiliations within his heart, regardless of his young age.

If things stopped at the beatings, things would have been a little better for Martin, but it's possible to imagine how he felt seeing other parents come and pick their kids up. As for him, he would go home alone, holding that backpack that hurt his shoulders. His step-mother had ordered the school to give him permission to walk home alone because their house was nearby, but the house was in fact, fifteen minutes away if you were to walk. It's unimaginable to see a little boy walking that distance even with the bad weather, including the bitter cold and the pouring rain, while carrying that heavy bag on his back.

It's normal to assume that Martin had no friends, for who would befriend such a stupid human being. Even walking besides him brought embarrassment among anyone who dared to do so, but that's for his life outside of his house.

At home, he is the son of a man who lives his late teenage years with his new wife, and his son was the last thing he thought of. With all of that, Martin wasn't a failure when it came to studying, nor was he a genius. He would study alone, and never did he dare to ask for help from anyone when studying or doing his homework.

When Martin turned eleven years old, on the night of Christmas to be exact; that night is known by many as the most wonderful time of the year. It's the atmosphere of beautiful family reunions and the presents for the children, all are memories that reside in everyone's heart, children or adults. Martin was at the house, in his room or be specific, as he was used to always. He never went out of the house except to go to school. He heard movements in the beneath him, downstairs, so he ran quickly there. He found his dad and his wife getting ready to leave; they were going to the movies then having dinner. Martin begged to go along, but his step mother yelled at him to shut up, and she ordered him to clean the house, even though he cleans it a thousand times a day, but it was just a foolish remark by her. Martin looked to his father as if to soften his heart, but his dad's answer was to back up his wife. He told him to clean the house and go to sleep.

The good thing is that Martin didn't know what today was, or what Christmas means, for he had never lived the experience. He went up to his room, that dark room. Martin never once opened the curtains that blocked the light, whether it was day or night. That night though, he headed toward the window and opened the curtain then proceeded with the window. That was the first time he did so; the cold breeze blew against his face as he closed his eyes.

He opened them to find the street and all of the houses decorated with all sorts of lights. The scene was amazing. Martin didn't know the reason behind that lighting. His attention focused on the house facing theirs, and he found a group of people standing at the door, young and old, in the middle of talks and laughter's. Especially that man with the white beard and the red hat and clothes; the one who carried the children on his back and took them into the house. That was a great atmosphere, an atmosphere that Martin was missing out on--the family, the love and care. At that moment, he decided to head out the window and go to that house because their door was locked as usual, and there was no escape but that window. That was the first time ever that Martin had run away from home. He was able to leave and walk to the house in front of them. He headed straight to the window and began spying. He saw big toys and teddy bears, and the children were playing and laughing. All of them surrounded by the guy who wore the red costume. He was the one giving them the gifts, and each one of them was lining up to receive their present. Martin lifted his hand and placed it on the window; he thought he was standing with them in line, waiting for his gift. At that moment, he asked himself one question: if my mother was still living, would this atmosphere be the same at our house?

Martin only looked through the window and looked around him; he found a small tree decorated with lights. He headed towards it and before he could even touch it, he heard a yell from behind. Martin got nervous and tried to escape, but the man who yelled told him to stop and said he won't hurt him. Martin stopped, but he was terrified. That man was the same one who was wearing the red costume, and he said:

"Where's your house?"

Martin pointed to his house while shaking and the man replied:

"You're Mr. Jeff's son! Where is your dad?"

Martin had to lie as he answered nervously:

"He went to get me a really big toy!"

He was motioning with his hands to show him how big that present was, which didn't even exist. The man knew Martin was lying because he saw his sorrowful looks when he looked through that window. That's why he came outside to find out the story behind that little boy; therefore, he didn't discuss much with him. He took off his hat and his white beard and gave them to Martin.

Martin took them without saying a single word; his eyes were still set on that little tree; the man noticed:

"Take it... It's yours."

Martin couldn't believe what the man said:

"Really?"

The man smiled:

"Yes, it's yours!"

Martin was beyond happy at that moment:

"Thank you! Thank you!"

He walked over to the tree and took it with him, but what did Martin want with that tree? Also, how will he be able to get it in the house if he had escaped without permission?

When Martin arrived at the house, he placed the hat, the white beard, and the tree aside, then, he went up to his room, looking for a flashlight. He found one and went back down, creeping through the window. When he reached the bottom, he wore the hat and put on the beard; he then fled.

Martin was racing time; even though the tree was small, it numbed his hands due to its heaviness, but he bore it because the place he was heading to was far more important, and he wanted to get back home before his dad and step-mother. He finally arrived to his desired destination; do you know what that place was? It was the graveyard where his mother was buried.

Night and cemetery-- is there anything scarier? Not for Martin; fear was his friend, and it's not possible for someone to fear their friend. He crept into the cemetery, and he knew where his mother's grave was because he had visited before, not many times, but those times were enough to leave the place in his memory. He turned the light on, and began lighting the way until he got to his mom's grave. He headed for the grave, sat beside it, and began talking to his mother. He didn't speak much of the days he spent with her because he hadn't spent much time with her. He didn't talk about what his dad and his step-mother did to him either, for he didn't want his mother to be sad. All he talked about was how much he loved her and missed her. When he finished talking, he got up and walked toward the tree and picked it up; he then began yelling and jumping likes a crazy person while telling his mom:

"I am the old man... I've brought you a present!"

The old man is Santa clause, whom Martin didn't know the name of. All he knew was that he was an old man. Neither did he know that the people were the ones who bring the trees and decorate them, not Santa, but how was Martin supposed to know all of those things?

It's now time for him to go home, even though he didn't want to. That night was the best night he has ever had; he understood the meaning of freedom and happiness while next to his mother, but he had to go back. He placed the tree next to her grave and took off his hat and put it at the edge of the grave marker along with the beard. He then said his goodbyes to his mom and headed for home.

To his bad luck, his father and his wife arrived to the house before him. They never made sure he was okay, nor did they go to his room to see him. That night though, his step-mother had to go up to his room because she found everything in its place, which means Martin didn't clean. She stormed to his room with fire burning from her eyes. She found the window open, and he wasn't there. That was the best thing for her because she wanted him to run away. Excited about that, she began searching for a letter to make sure, but she was surprised while opening one of the drawers with a drawing that he had painted. When she saw it, her hands shook, not of fear, but of anger. The drawing was of a man with a snake suffocating him, almost breaking his bones. There was a small boy holding a sword, and on the man, he wrote that it was his father, and the snake was his wife; the little boy was Martin himself. That drawing explained its self and what Martin was feeling. That poor kid knew nothing of what was waiting for him at the house.

Martin appeared at the window suddenly, and he was surprised to see his step-mother, who was still in his room. In return, she was also shocked to see him, since she thought he had ran away, but she was also glad he came back so that she can let out the fire burning inside of her due to that drawing. Martin noticed that she had the drawing in her hands, and he knew exactly what was going to happen. With an angry tone and an evil look, she said:

"Wait here!"

For Martin, there was nothing he can do but to sit at that corner, where he had spent most of his time, and prepare for the torture. He placed his head between his legs and closed them with his arms, making him look appear as a snail going back into its shell. His step-mother came back, holding a rubber water hose that's used for watering the plants, and she said as she looked at him:

"What do you think of this snake you fool?"

She began furiously beating him, and there was something making her beat him stronger each time: Martin, for the first time, didn't scream or feel painful. All that was happening to him was the movement of his body because of the power of each blow.

As for her, she was yelling and cursing; her noisy voice was loud enough for the dad to hear and come running to Martin's room. He saw her abusing him and asked her for the reason; she gave him the drawing, and he moved her back as her pulled out his belt and said:

"And what do you think of this snake!"

Martin was still sitting the same, but he knew what the snake his dad has; it was his belt, the one that he had been beaten with many times. His dad took over to finish what his wife had started; with each strike, Martin's body would shake, but there was no mercy whatsoever.

Martin's eyes were closed, in pain, but what happened at the graveyard and with that man; all of those thing were like an anesthetic needle against those strikes. Those memories were what he thought of at that moment, and he didn't want for the abuse to ruin that beautiful night.

The torture ended, and he was capable of running away, but he didn't; he was very patient and held on.

Martin's life didn't change much when he turned twenty-one. He was coming back from college when he heard yelling coming from the house, so he immediately headed inside. For the first time, his dad and his step-mother were fighting, and beside his dad stood a strange man. Martin was listening to what went on, and from what he heard, it seemed like his dad had given ownership of the house to his step-mother, doing so, she asked for a divorce and told him that he must leave the house. The strange man was her lover. Everything is lost, his dad thought, when he fell down to the ground due to a heart attack. His step mother asked Martin to carry his dad and get out of the house.

That woman was cooking the dish of evilness at a low heat until she gained what she wants and kicked both of them out. Martin couldn't do anything but carry his dad to the hospital. He left the college and start working two shifts in order to pay for his dad's treatment, and his father was still under the influence of that heart attack, which could potentially end his life. Why does Martin do all of that for his dad? There is no answer but the fact that it was his dad."

The arrow turned and chose Samantha, and the old woman began:

CHAPTER 7

SAMANTHA

"Samantha, a twenty-two year old, has a bachelor's degree in arts with a perfect score. She loved everything about arts; such as: sculpting and painting. She may seem familiar to you, so I'll have you know, she is Samantha the model; do you remember her?

She is not the same girl she was a month before now. Samantha is the owner of the most beautiful face you can ever seem, and the wonderful shape. What you see now is nothing but a girl whose bones are almost showing, as if she is a live ghost.

Her attractive beauty was the main reason that made her a famous model; as all of you know, whatever product she endorses, including those with bad quality, she can turn them into diamonds.

What many don't know is that Samantha is very sensitive; she is more sensitive than little kids. People looked to her as an arrogant and selfish person because of her beauty and fame. It wasn't the truth; the situation is similar to a desert that's covered in snow, but the people's eyes looked at the desert, ignoring the whiteness of the snow which was her heart.

It was natural for guys to be attracted to her; even if she wasn't a model, her beauty was enough to make all of them her slaves, but Samantha didn't rush, especially with the nature of her work and her business with the world of fashion and advertisements. Although, that doesn't mean she hasn't thought of being in relationship with someone she loves. She had drawn a mental image of her "prince charming"; his looks or his social class didn't matter; all she looked for was a person who shares the same interests as her; in one word-- understanding.

There was a park that Samantha usually went to daily. There, she felt peace and serenity, far away from lights and the noises. That beautiful park with its quietness and the gentle breezes of air, along with the wonderful scent of flowers. If you heard one sound at that place, be sure that it's the chirping of birds; that's why Samantha loved the place dearly.

One day, Samantha was sitting on the long bench at that park; that day she was in deep thought, admiring the beautiful scenery and delighting her ears with the singing of those birds, until a man sat by her; she didn't pay attention to his approach, so he began:

"This place is the most beautiful place in the world.. Here you feel peace, away from the noise of the outside world."

Samantha suddenly jumped, for that man took away her deep thinking, but he took notice of that and quickly apologized. The smile never left that man's face, so she exchanged the same smile:

"You're right! It's the most beautiful place in the world!"

The man extended his hand, introducing himself:

"By the way, I am Michael."

She shook his hand, still smiling:

"..And I am Samantha."

"What's the nature of your work?" He questioned. "Seems like you don't read much magazines or newspapers."

"Well, no. I am not a big fan; sometimes I read the sports' section or the weather, but that's about it. Why do you ask though? Are you a journalist?"

Samantha laughed: "No, I am a model."

"Wow! Why I am not surprised."

Samantha's face turned red because of Michael's compliment, and she smiled shyly. In return, she asked about his nature of work, and he told her that he worked at one of the companies in the morning, and afterwards, he goes to his small place where he pursues his hobby of sculpting.

Samantha was filled with happiness because she loves these things. She told him that she has a bachelor's degree in arts; he smiled and told her she was joking, but she told him that she also wanted to visit his place, and he loved the idea. He would be more than happy if she visited his small, humble place.

Their conversation lasted, about artists and sculptors. Each of them had excellent information about such topic, or at least enough for the conversation to last an hour. When you find a person who has the same interests, it becomes difficult to stop talking, not for a while at least.

After their long talks, they both stopped talking for a minute, and Michael began:

"Do you know that there is something missing right now?"

She answered: "what's that?"

"It's hot chocolate!" He continued.

"Hahaha. You're impossible!"

"Why?"

"Because I am used to drinking hot chocolate every time I come here, but my conversation with you made me forget!"

Michael smiled and joked: "You're just copying me miss! Alright, I am going to get you the hot chocolate."

"No... I am coming with you!"

Both of them went to the cafe nearby and ordered the hot chocolate. Then, they walked back to the bench; on the way, Samantha mentioned:

"You know. I don't remember a day when I didn't come here; I've always come here."

"That's my bad luck. I've always came here, but this is the first time I've seen you here; I think our times may have been completely different."

Both smiled, and it was now time to leave. Michael wrote his place's address on the napkin and handed it to Samantha, and he told her that he will be anxiously waiting. In return, she promised to call him when she decides to come.

Throughout the trip back home, Samantha thought of him. Could it really be a coincidence? That strange understanding between them, his sudden appearance? It's far more than just a coincidence; it's fate that wanted her to meet him. That's what she was thinking.

Two days only until Samantha called Michael and informed him that she was coming; upon her arrival, she was overflowing with happiness while looking at the sculptors and the art pieces.

Since then, Samantha and Michael began going out every day, and if she didn't see him, she would talk to him on the phone. That sort of thing helped her recover more of his interests, which she shared the same of, and that made become closer. Only to turn the stage of admiration and understanding into love.

Samantha had a friend named Sara; she knew everything about Samantha because she was her childhood friend. Samantha told her about Michael, and she was very happy for her, but she also encouraged her to love him more. She also warned her not to lose him because simply, he was her "prince charming".

Today is Samantha's birthday; she couldn't sleep whatsoever that night. All of her thought was focused on what Michael was going to do for her, for the first occasion is always the most special in any relationship. The first occasion is the one where the person tries to show the amount of love. Love at that stage is at the age of sprouts. During that special occasion, know that you won't be able to forget, not even the smallest of details; everything will remain with the memories forever.

The thoughts were roaming in her head; the thing she thought of mostly was that his gift would be a wedding ring. Even though their relationship didn't even exceed six months, but love knows no boundaries or time limits.

The meeting place, as usual, was the park where they met the first time. Samantha came one hour ahead of time because she was eager to know what will take place, or what Michael was going to do. Michael arrived, and with each step, her heart was beating faster, but when she looked at him, he had nothing in his hands. She told herself that it was surely going to be the ring, and it's in his pocket, but when she looked at him, she saw that for the first time he wasn't smiling; instead he was gloomy-faced. He sat by her, but he didn't look at her or say a word beside "hello".

That was the first shock, but she smiled nervously and waited for him to say or do something. Instead; Michael was like the chair he was sitting on; he didn't move or say a single word. Samantha reminded him:

"Today is my birthday."

He turned to her and replied with coldness and plainly without even meaning it:

"Really... well happy birthday."

He then turned back around and looked at the park; that was the second shock, in such short time. Those words were similar to a bolt of thunder to her heart; that surprise cause a short paralysis.

Were there other surprises in store? Samantha wished that it had stopped at that, but Michael didn't stop at that; he continued:

"Listen... It seems like things went way too fast; I didn't think you'd be that easy. As for the similar interests we had, that were nothing but lies. I don't like arts, or even know anything about them. I don't love you, and I never will. I've found another woman who's much more compatible with me. I am sorry, and I wish you the best of luck."

He then got up and left the park. We can say that a cold bucket of water and ice had been dumped on Samantha. I find that relation to be a failure to describe what she actually felt at that moment. There are many questions surrounding what he had just said. His words indicate that he knew exactly who she was and what she loved. It also seemed as if had been dared to win her heart, and that he won easily.

Samantha wasn't even thinking of that, she wasn't there anyways; she was still under the effect of that shock. Her eyes widened, and tears began to flood down from her eyes.

Can you imagine to have drawn the most beautiful images in your mind, and at such a special day in your life, only to be surprised with the exact opposite? To expect a red rose, but instead receive a knife to stab you in the heart? Samantha had no idea that the place she thought she was born again at will be the place of her death.

She went back home, not knowing how she got there. That body was still walking without a soul; she locked herself in her room, and she didn't eat anything or leave here room. She also ignored everything that had to do with the companies, advertisements, or anything that was tied with the world outside. She never even left the bed; all she did was cry all day, and she attempted suicide several times, but she failed. Her mom was then forced to keep a closer eye on her, Samantha remained like that for two weeks, and Sara always visited her to make sure she was okay and help ease her pain.

Along with her mom, Sara tried to convince her to go out because being alone only made things worse; going out might change things up for her a little. Despite all of their tries ending up in failure, Samantha finally agreed to go out with her mother, who told her that she would only take her out in the care, and they wouldn't have to get out.

Samantha went out with her mother, and her mom was the one driving. They came close to the park. All Samantha could do was to cover her ears because when they got near it, she remembered the last meeting she had with Michael, and his voice was still talking to her as if she was living the situation again. She immediately yelled at her mother, but her mother wasn't paying attention to what was going on because she was focused on driving:

"Hurry... Hurry... I want to go back home!" Samantha yelled repeatedly.

Her mother was surprised, and she could do nothing but to listen to her daughter's request. She turned again and headed for the house. There was no other way but downtown; the roads were very busy, and the car was barely moving. Samantha raised her head to look around and make sure that they passed the park, but she wished that she hadn't. While looking, she saw at one of the cafe's, with glass windows, Michael sitting there; that wasn't the only thing that cause her a complete meltdown, but the person who accompanied him-- it was her childhood friend, Sara.

Samantha fainted because of that huge shock, which she couldn't handle. She fell to the side on her mother, who was too busy driving with all the cars around. The mother freaked out, seeing her daughter fall on her, and she tried to wake her up, but to know avail. She then called the ambulance because she didn't know how to act in these situations; she was just overwhelmed with nerves; you can almost hear the sound of her bones shivering fearfully.

She was taken to the hospital and went back to her bedroom, the only place where she currently felt safe. Samantha completely gave up, for she was a failure at love, a failure at suicide, and all of these things had chosen a slow death for her; she anxiously waited for death. No one wished to die more than Samantha."

The arrow turned, and it was Jessica's turn this time; soon after it stopped, the old woman started:

CHAPTER 8

―――――――――――

JESSICA

"Jessica, a seventeen year old girl; she is the youngest here. She may not be the hero of this story, but what happened to her is a tragedy no girl her age could handle. She is a high school student, and she was very spoiled, especially by her brother, William, with whom she shared a very strong relationship. Jessica lived in a farm at one of the countryside's along with her family which consisted of four members: her mother, her father, her brother, and her. Their income was very limited and simple; they can be considered poor. Despite those difficult circumstances, Jessica never felt like she was lacking anything because William offered her the most wonderful life. To him, she was more than a sister; she was like a daughter he didn't have.

Of course, with harvesting and farming, you can't be sure of what will happen because it's always changing. Because of this family's poorness and the economic crisis that had taken place; all of these factors contributed to the collapse of their farm, and it didn't bring any income at all. Instead, they were paying more than the farm produced for them. Petroleum prices on the rise, labor workers, and farming tools-- all of these factors didn't care for the livingness' and loyalty, but they only understood one thing-- money and money was not available. The family's situation deteriorated terribly until they went under the poverty line. Jessica's father decided to sell the farm, which he dearly loved. To him, it was more than just a regular farm; he considered it a treasure that has been handed down to him from his ancestors, and he thought of it as a heart-breaking decision to fail in keeping a family's treasure, but life didn't care about these matters.

A few days after the farm was put up for sale; a stranger came by the family's house in the hopes of buying their farm. The strange man was welcomed by the father and they came to a complete deal enclosure; all there was left to do is sign the official documents.

Jessica was still a baby at the time, for she hadn't even reached three years of age yet, but William was thirteen. He was standing by his dad, who held the pen to sign that contract, but his hands were shaking, as if he was about to sign the certificate of his death. William was looking at his father's hand shaking; he then looked to his eyes and found them sparkling from tears, until a tear fell down on the paper.

Do you know what the hardest thing a son can see during his lifetime? Seeing his father weak and crying; William despised seeing his dad in that situation, so he grabbed the paper and tore it to pieces; he then looked at the man and said:

"Sorry sir, but this farm is not for sale! Thank you for coming."

When the stranger looked into William's eyes, he knew that he was being serious, so he looked at his father, who had lowered his head, as if he had admired what his son just did; the one thing he couldn't do himself.

The man now knew that a deal will not be reached; he immediately got up and left, without bothering to say a single word. As for William, he put his hand on his father's shoulder:

"I am sorry... But I promise you, I will bring back life to this farm, but you also have to promise me something."

The dad looked at William and saw the determination in the eyes of that kid, who hasn't even reached thirteen, yet he was speaking the words of a brave man, and his dad looked to him:

"I promise you anything you want, without even knowing what it is."

William smiled at his dad's words and hugged him tightly. What he felt that night is indescribable. It's unconditional trust. How beautiful it is to know that the people around you believe in you and trust you.

That promise was to let William do whatever he please. That day, William decided to leave school and put all of his time and energy into the farm. He worked at the farm from dawn to dusk, and when the sun went down, he would go work at the gas station nearby until midnight. He got there by walking, and it was about half an hour away by foot.

Little William knew not the meaning of sleep or rest; he only slept three hours at the maximum. The small amount of money he received from the gas station went to the farm and his family. As for himself, he never even took one dollar.

He had to sacrifice his childhood for his family, who were on the verge of becoming homeless. He also spent the money on Jessica, so she wouldn't need anything, as if he didn't want her to live the same life he was living. Jessica's happiness and smile gave him the most hope and encouragement to work harder.

William worked at the farm under all conditions; while he was sick, even under the pouring rain. When it rained, William worked in his dirty clothes, which were the only ones he wore. He would look at sky and cry, asking God to stand by him. Those raindrops always hid his tears. As if they didn't want him to cry.

Despite all of these difficult times William was going through, his smile never left his face, and even though he didn't have enough time, he always took Jessica with him to the pond near their farm. He played with her and taught her how to fish, despite his weakness and tiredness. The sound of Jessica's laughter's made him forget all of that. When it was her birthday, William gifted her small boat that he had made himself, just for her. All of that, and his family never heard him complain once.

As for his parents, they helped when they could because they weren't young, and they weren't able to work as much as William. Even with his disagreement about the idea of his parents working with him at the farm, they insisted, so he didn't want to disobey them.

All the hard work William performed began recovering the farm, but not to an excellent level; it was now capable of paying off a few of its debts, and he was able to lift his family from under the poverty line.

That was William's life; a farmer in the morning and a worker at night. When Jessica turned sixteen, he knew that things weren't going to go very well. Jessica was now only steps away from college, which meant he needed more money to cover the needs of that teenage girl, in order for her to live a normal life that any girl her age would be living. He began thinking of ways to get the money he needed.

William heard that there were deployments for the military; he would have to go to Iraq for two years and come back; that was a great opportunity with a large amount of money. All the money he gets would be given to his dad, and he would provide for his family's future. That was the best solution that would solve all his problems, including the farm. He can even hire workers for it, and generating a descent amount of money to bring back life to that farm.

That was the only chance and the best solution. That's what William was thinking, and he applied for it, but he didn't tell anyone about it, until he was sure of his departure. It was only a short while until he received a reply telling him to get ready to go to Iraq.

Now William had to go back and tell his parents of what he was planning to do. He gathered them and informed them of his intention to go to Iraq and come back two years later. His mother cried, while his dad was in total shock. Rejection was their answer, but he kept trying to convince them of the fact that this would insure their future, but to no avail. His mother was telling him that they want to give him money in the place of his life. William was not young, he was almost thirty, and he wasn't married, nor had he even lived a full life. Until when is he going to sacrifice himself for us; he has to leave them and live the rest of his life with happiness. Thos were the words of his mother, who was still crying.

William wasn't really affected by his mother's words; instead, he looked at his dad:

"Do you remember your promise to me when I was little?"

How can his dad forget that promise? He had grabbed the arm that hurts the most, and his dad couldn't answer. He was lost between his son and the promise he would break. He is in a situation that no one could envy. When he looked into William's eyes, he saw determination, as if the time had gone back to when he was younger; after the silence, the father asked:

"Is that what you really want?"

"Yes. That's what I want; please don't break your promise," William replied without hesitation.

"Then you can do what you want," his dad finished; he then got up from his chair and headed straight to the door. His wife began shouting that he couldn't do that; to sacrifice his son for the sake of money, even though that wasn't the reason, but if he couldn't stand in a child's face, how can he stand to him when he is an adult? It was trust and given responsibility. William also asked his dad not to tell Jessica of this; he asked him to tell her that he was going to work anywhere, not Iraq. He was barely finished until he heard the sound of someone's feet hitting the wooden floors strongly. Those steps indicated that someone was running from something; they were Jessica's steps, who heard everything from behind the door and took off running while crying. William found out, and yelled nervously:

"Oh my God!! Jessica... No!!"

She heard the truth, and William chased her at the speed of lighting. It wasn't hard for him to find her; she was at that pond where the both of them had always met. He walked closer to her, trying to talk to her. She was crying and didn't want to talk to him. He tried, but his attempts failed. He knew that he wasn't welcomed there, so he left.

The next day was the day of his departure; he was wearing his military uniform, ready to leave. He was ready for the unknown trip... He could come back or not. He went to say goodbye to his parents. Oh how difficult it is to say goodbye, for it could be the last time they see him. Between the hugs, tears, and cries, that was the atmosphere at their house. It was now time to leave; he must head to the pond to see Jessica, whom he loved more than anything in the world.

He arrived at the pond, and she still refused to talk to him, but he sat next to her and said:

"I know I am not wanted here, but I didn't lie because you were young and wouldn't understand. I just didn't want to see you cry, and I've done everything in my will to not see your tears. How do you think it would be if I was the one causing them? All I want to say is that I am in deep pain for leaving you guys, and I love you all so much. I have no idea how the seconds will pass away from you because I am not used to that. I will miss this pond and sitting here with you, but I promise you... I will come back... I promise."

He then got up and moved closer to her, trying to kiss her forehead, but he was shocked to see her move away. He was a bit let down because she hadn't understood what he was doing, and why he was doing it. He left, deeply hurt, and sadness would be the least to describe what he felt.

William left and the smile left that farm. It was destined to slowly die; no one talked or laughed. That farm became similar to a cemetery, or even an abandoned cave, so to speak. He would send money to the, and he also called them, but no one besides his dad wanted to talk to him, which forced his dad to lie and tell him that they were not at the farm. William knew that has dad been lying and that his mother and sister were still mad at him. This situation was very painful for him because he was in the utmost need of hearing their voices during his alienation, which almost suffocated him to death.

Scary darkness settled on that farm, and in the center of that farm was a small candle that lit up the whole place. That candle was the hope of William's return, but the wind doesn't recognize those feelings. It blew strongly from the gates of that farm, turning that little candle off. William died, and that wind was the general from the military who came to inform the family of the tragedy and give them that flag.

The shock was huge; the mother couldn't handle the news, and she fainted. His father stepped back from the surprise, and he couldn't balance himself. Jessica took off insanely running; she would fall down, get up, and continue running. Until she arrived at the pond, as if she had thought that William was going to be there. It was bitter cold that night; Jessica fell down to her knees and loudly cried:

"Why? Why?? You promised you'd come back, but you didn't keep your promise."

These words came straight from her heart to the person she loved the most. She suddenly got up and headed closer to the pond, walking into the waters, step by step. The water was freezing, but she couldn't feel it; the news of William's death had paralyzed her senses. She walked deeper into water until it reached her neck. She wanted to commit suicide to follow her brother; she imagined him standing at the end of the pond; he was telling her:

"Go back... They need you."

Those were the words Jessica heard; she closed her eyes, but quickly opened them to look again, but she found nothing this time. She was sure she had seen William and heard his voice, but she decided to go back.

Everything ended; happiness didn't have a place at the farm. Yes, it generated more from the money William sent, but what good is that when the soul of that farm had died?

That family's life became very miserable; the father would sit in the center of the farm for hours and refused to talk to anyone. All he would do is picture his son working at that farm. The mother never left bed after receiving the news; she would hold his picture close to her heart and cry. As for Jessica, she never left that pond at anytime."

The arrow spun again, choosing Kevin this time, which meant another story for the old woman to tell:

CHAPTER 9

KEVIN

"Kevin-- it seems like he is the oldest by the way he looks. He has gray hair and wrinkles, but allow me to tell you that he is only in his thirty's." She introduced.

"Kevin lived a normal life; he searched for happiness, to find whoever his heart chooses, and to have children. He lost his father at a young age, and he lived with his mother, who took very good care of him. She loved him greatly, and she gave up all her time to compensate the place of his father. She gave up everything in her life to make that come true; be sure that she succeeded at that!

Kevin was able to receive a bachelor's degree in law, and he became a lawyer. He was still living with his mother. He loved her and knew all the credit goes to that great mother, and no matter what he does, he can't ever repay her.

He had two friends, David and Diana. David was his childhood friend, while Diana was his girlfriend, whom he loved very much, and they shared an amazing love story.

That story ended with Kevin marrying her, but there was something he didn't know. David loved Diana also. Even before she got married, he tried getting closer to her. She knew, and she in return turned him away, but she never told Kevin. How can she tell him that his closest friend loves her, and he encourages her to leave Kevin and marry him instead? That's why she decided to work with the situation hoping that David would leave her alone, but that didn't happen, even after she got married.

Kevin worked at an elite law office because he didn't have enough money to create his own private office. His married life was excellent, but it lacked one thing--children. Kevin and Diana didn't have any kids; they weren't sterile, but they had a small problem. That's why they were undergoing treatment in the hopes of having children someday. According to the doctor, the situation is difficult, but it's not impossible. The important thing is that they continue treatment. Kevin always dreamed of having kids, and he would tell Diana that she will have a boy. He didn't pressure her with this kind of talk, but he truly believed it. Even though they've been married for five years, they weren't blessed with a single child, not even a signal or sign that it was going to happen.

One day, Kevin's boss informed him that he has a case for him that can transform his life. His boss favored him, so he wanted to give Kevin that golden chance to express his appreciation for Kevin's hard work, and Kevin was also one of the few who deserves to see the light.

That case was in another state, which meant Kevin would have to leave for two months. Of course he didn't reject the offer because it's a once in a lifetime deal. To become a famous lawyer and have your own office--it's the dream of every lawyer. He went back to tell his wife and his mother, and they were very content to hear the news, and they encouraged him to take it. Diana asked to attend with him, but he refused because he didn't want to leave his mother alone, and Diana had to stay with her. Diana didn't mind at all because not only was she her mother-in-law, but she was also like a mother to her.

Kevin traveled to the future waiting for him, hoping to come back with good news. As for David, that was his chance, for he hadn't lost hope. He began following Diana; not only that, but he even began regularly visiting their house, with the excuse of making sure they're okay because he was a family friend, but Diana was smart, and she was completely ready for him. She never left the house, and she never saw him when he visited. She wouldn't answer his calls; all in an attempt to keep danger away from that man.

The time period for Kevin's deal passed. He hit huge success, and life smiled to him, announcing a brighter future. Today is Kevin's return day; he came back through the airport and then boarded a train to his town, knowing that Diana would be waiting for him outside. He had greatly missed her, and he was thinking of ways to show that. Even though it was only two months, but it's love.

Kevin exited from the station, and he looked left and right until he found Diana parking her car at the further lot. She had to park there because she couldn't find another space with all the congestion. He smiled at her and wave, in return, she also smiled. She was holding a white paper in her hands, and she seemed very happy. In fact, because she was too overwhelmed, she didn't think to look for oncoming cars, but Kevin saw a car coming in at an insane speech; he yelled:

"Diana! Look out!"

His words weren't able to stop what happened; Diana suddenly stopped watching that car fastly coming at her. The car hit her and threw her several meters away.

That scene was slower than a turtle for Kevin, as he saw Diana fly in the air. To top it off, the person who was driving the car was his childhood friend, David, who stared at Kevin after hitting her.

Kevin didn't know why he did that, but you all know it was revenge. It's like he was saying that if he can't have Diana then no one can.

David quickly took off, but Kevin was in complete shock. In insanity, he ran to her. All the cars were moving away from him, but he didn't care until he reached her; she was taking her last breath, and her blood had almost filled the street.

Kevin was yelling at the people around him to call the ambulance, and he was talking to Diana, telling her to hold on, but she wanted to talk, and she couldn't. She moved closer to him, and whispered:

"I am sorry."

Kevin had no clue why she said that, but she held up that hand that had the white paper in it; despite the strength of that hit and her weakness, she held on to that paper with all the strength she had left in her, as if that paper was more important than her life. Kevin grabbed that paper and read it; what that letter contained was happy news, but today, it was the worst news for him.

That paper said that Diana was pregnant; Kevin looked at her, but she had passed away. He tried to wake her up, but to no avail. He held her tightly to his chest and yelled; I'd never heard such a strong cry in my whole life; his vocal cords could have been cut due to the power of that scream. It was even heard by the people in the heavens; it was the name of Diana.

At that moment, the weather was just perfect, but it seems like that cry put the sky in tears. Suddenly, it started to heavily rain, and the raindrops took away Kevin's tears away, as it washed Diana's blood on the street.

Kevin was now like a body without its soul. The black under his eyes, the dilation of his eyes, the beard that covered his face and the paleness of his face-- all of these things could make you think you're standing in front of an insane person.

He never left his room, nor did he eat or talk. He was a prisoner of that room for a week. All of these things were noticed by his mother, who suffered deeply, seeing him in that state of being, and for losing his wife and his unborn child.

One week later, his mother was amazed to see him come out of his room, and he was smiling and talking to her normally as if nothing had happened. She was very shocked to see that; yes she was happy, and she didn't think it wouldn't happen that fast. She didn't pay much attention to it because she was just overwhelmed to see her son surpass that stage of depression.

That same night, at midnight, the mother heard a loud scream that made her jump out of bed. That was Kevin's voice, who was calling her to his room. She ran as fast as her legs could carry her to his room, and she found him on the side of the bed, and he seemed very nervous; he said:

"Hurry... Come help me... Diana is giving birth!"

It was a huge astonishment for her. Diana died, and no one was in that bed, but he yelled again telling her to hurry up and not just stand there. She saw how serious he was while talking, so what can she do? It's a mother's heart; she had to go along with the illusions her son created. She walked to the bed and acted like she was pulling the baby out; she was a great actress, and she mumbled:

"Come on... His head is out... He is almost here."

She did that while in tears, but Kevin reached his hand to the imaginary place where the baby was supposed to be, and he whispered:

"Look how beautiful he is... It's a boy... I told you would have a boy!"

He picked up that non-existent baby, and held it closer:

"My god! How beautiful he is!"

His mother was still stunned, as she saw her only son lose his mind, but Kevin quickly interrupted her thoughts:

"Mom, why aren't you answering? Diana is thanking you for helping her!"

She looked at him, and she was still crying. She then turned to look at the bed:

"No need to thank me darling."

Kevin then continued:

"Don't be sad Diana. My mother is crying because she is happy. She has waited for this child more than me!"

As for his mother, she got up and wanted to leave. She was lost and completely startled. When she arrived to the door, she heard Kevin yell:

"Don't you want to hold your grandson?"

She stopped and walked back to him. She reached out her arms to hold that illusion baby. She carried air, and she kissed air, and all of that was for Kevin. She didn't want to stun him with reality, while seeing him at the height of happiness.

Yes, those happenings made his mother have a complete meltdown, but she had to endure and be patience, for Kevin needed her badly. She began watching her son, dying a thousand times each day. She would secretly look into his room because he never left. That room was like the whole world to him, and she would see her son playing the "Secret Garden" on the piano, which was the music Diana always played for him. Kevin played that tune for his wife and his son to help them fall asleep, that's what his mother found out by watching him every day.

She decided to go in while he played that song one day, and while he played it, he felt his mom's present and said:

"Look at them mom; they're like angels in their sleep."

She answered:

"Yes, they are."

She wasn't looking at the bed, but at Kevin, meaning that he is the angel, not them.

The mother never thought of sending him to a mental hospital. Is there a mother who would do that to her only son? It's terrible, what's happening to Kevin, but to her it's better than seeing him at a mental hospital. Besides, it's all just nothing but imagination, and nothing dangerous was taking place. The kitchen, for Kevin, was one of the restaurants. The house was like a whole new world to him, that's why he never left the house.

One cold night, it was heavily raining. The mother went to look for Kevin in his room, but she couldn't find him. She was terrified, and she looked for him all around the house, but he was nowhere to be found. She began crying, worried about Kevin, for he wasn't mentally stabled, and the weather was frightening. Surely he was in danger: that's what that poor mother was thinking, but she suddenly heard Kevin laughing and talking outside. The voice was coming from their front yard; she quickly ran to the window and found him pushing the empty swing; amongst the laughter, he said:

"I am going to push it harder this time!"

You can understand that Kevin thought Diana and his son were in that swing, and he was playing with him. Despite the heavy rains, he cared only about playing with his family.

His mother looked out that window in a complete state of shock; what else can she do? She watched as Kevin suddenly stopped and opened an umbrella; he began walking away from the house.

He didn't use that umbrella to protect himself; instead, he was protecting his wife and child. As for himself, he was under the rain; his mother had to follow him, and she quickly left to catch him and took another umbrella with her.

Kevin walked toward the unknown, that's what it seemed to his mother, but for him, he knew exactly where he was going.

She followed him without letting him take notice; he walked with a smile painted on his face, as he talked to Diana, who didn't exist. People pointed at him, and they laughed loudly. Others looked at him, and made fun of him because Kevin held the umbrella next to him, protecting the air, while he was soaking in water. What made them laugh also, was that old woman that walked behind him.

He personally didn't care, and he didn't know what they were laughing about. In his eyes, there wasn't anything funny; he was only holding that umbrella to protect his wife and son from the rain.

The sound of those laughter's pierced through his mother's ears though; they were like a knife stabbing her heart, as she saw people laughing and making fun of her son. It's the most difficult thing a mother has to endure in the world.

Kevin suddenly stopped at one of the stores; it was a kid's store, and he pointed at the showcase behind the glass windows of that store. He was pointing at a baby bed, which he seemed to like, and Diana agreed. He walked into the store and bought that bed; he then came back out and held the umbrella with his left hand and the bed with his right.

His mother hid, so that Kevin wouldn't notice her, and she followed him until he arrived him and went straight back to his room.

It was very hard for the mother; she was in huge confusion. What will she do? She decided to call her sister and inform her of what's happening. Her sister quickly came to see what was going on, and she took her to Kevin's room, slightly opened the door, and showed her what he was doing.

Kevin's aunt didn't expect to see what she saw; yes she knew what was happening, but she didn't know it had gone that far.

She saw Kevin playing the usual song of the piano, as he talked to his son, who was sitting in his lab:

"You must learn this song because when you get older, you have to play it for your mother and me when we go to sleep."

When he finished, he said:

"Today's lesson has ended my son; you have to sleep now."

So he took that child and put him in his new bed, and he began singing him lullabies.

His mother collapsed, and she buried her head between her hands as she cried, while her sister couldn't believe what's happening. As his mother cried:

"What can I do? What should I do?'

Her sister took her downstairs, and she told her that she must send him to the mental hospital. She was angered by the proposal and rejected it, but her sister insisted. She told her that if anything happened to Kevin, she would be responsible, but all her tries failed.

The mother came up with a plan that she wanted to carry out. She decided that morning to go to Kevin's room, and she told him that she wanted him to go with her somewhere. He didn't have a problem with it, and he asked Diana to come, but his mother told him in a strict voice that she wanted him alone. He agreed, and they went out alone.

They arrived at the spot; it was the place where Diana died; she asked him:

"Does this place remind you of something?"

After a deep though, Kevin's reply was:

"No..."

She insisted:

"Focus more... Does this place remind you of something?"

He smiled:

"I told you know, why?"

She didn't answer him and ordered him to follow her. Kevin walked behind her, not knowing what's going on. He just followed his mother's orders.

This time, she took him to the graveyard, specifically, at Diana's grave. She stopped there and pointed:

"Look!"

Kevin looked at it, but it wasn't a deep look:

"What's this?"

"This is your wife's grave!"

He busted out in laughter:

"My wife's grave? The one who's at home now with my child?'

He was surprised with that hand that came and strongly slapped him. That was the first time his mother had hit him; she cried:

"Wake up! Your wife died, and you don't have a child!"

It was a huge shock for Kevin; he couldn't believe her. He pushed his mother to the ground and yelled:

"You're crazy! If you don't want us at your house, we're leaving!"

He walked over to that identifier and kicked it also to the ground, as he continued:

"Seems like you're getting old, and you've lost your mind!"

Yes, he was crying while he did that. He took off running as if he was escaping. Kevin thought his family was in danger from his mother, and he went to rescue them.

It's very painful for the mother to have Kevin push her and describe her as "insane", but what she feared more was Kevin. He is in danger, and he is running to the unknown. She had to do something that she didn't want at all, or she didn't even imagine she would do so some day; she called the mental hospital.

The hospital workers arrived to the house, and Kevin was taking the clothes and yelling:

"Hurry, we have to leave now!"

He was talking to Diana, but they caught him, and put him in that white straightjacket as he yelled:

"Let me go! Why are you doing this to me?!"

His mother just arrived at the house to witness that horrible scene, and her son who cried for her help. Not this time: that's what his mother said to herself.

Kevin was taken to the mental hospital, and they tied him to the bed to restrict his movement. He was put in a white room that was cut off from everything. It contained nothing but that bed and that glass, medium-sized square, which the observation room was behind, where his mother and doctor stood, looking at his condition.

Kevin yelled:

"Let me go! Today is Kevin's birthday...I promised to take him to Disney Land!"

Nick was the name he picked for his son that wasn't born, and Disney Land was that swing at their house.

Kevin began getting weak and losing hope, for he was tied in place with no movement, and no one came for help. He calmed down suddenly and looked out that small window as if he had known they were watching. That tear fell from his dilated eyes, as he quietly said:

"Why are you doing this to us? Diana always told me that she really loved you, and nick too. Why mom? Why?"

His mother witnessed as she exploded in tears like a child. The doctor reached his hand to wipe the tears from behind his glasses. To be a doctor at a mental hospital doesn't mean you don't have emotions or feelings... The doctor walked to the crying mother, and he tried to calm her down. Seeing a mother in that condition is something that can cause goose bumps. He promised her that he would do everything in his power to bring Kevin back."

She finished, but the arrow didn't need to spin this time, for no one else was left but John.

CHAPTER 10

JOHN

"John is the last one; he is counted as the oldest here, for he is thirty-six years old. He couldn't finish his education due to his family's difficult conditions. He had to work to help his family, and his family consisted of: his parents, him, and his brothers. It's not true to say that John has a specific job, because he works at any job he meets. Whenever he is offered a higher pay, he headed in the direction of that offer.

When John reached twenty-five years of age, he decided to marry that woman he met one day. Their relationship became stronger, and that's when he decided to marry her.

One day, John heard about a chance to move to America, and that there is a better job for him there. It would give him a much better life than the one he is living, and it would help him ensure the future of his kids.

He discussed the issue with his family and wife, and they agreed. His brothers were not young anymore, and they can find a way to help their parents. John also had to live his own life and carry out the responsibilities of his wife and children.

John did just that; he emigrated here with his wife. He began working hard with his wife to fight for their living. Everything was going fine, and his wife had two beautiful girls. John didn't know that this was the signal of a future curse.

Their spending increased, and they weren't able to afford all of their needs. The kids, the house, and all of that were much more than their monthly income.

When poorness enters a house, be sure that chaos and trouble will take over. That's exactly what happened with John; his wife began complaining. She started saying that she can't live that life of poverty, and that John was spending all of their money on the girls, which made her very angry. As if the kids weren't her children too. John justified that it was all for the girls, and that he would do much more if it were in his hands.

The young wife didn't appreciate that, and she asked for a divorce. John tried everything possible to change her mind, at least for their daughters, but she had her mind set and insisted on a divorce. When he saw that she wasn't going to change her mind, he agreed less than one condition, which was for her to leave the girls. That poor guy didn't know that it was the best thing she had heard; she wanted to live the life of teenagers, and who would want her if she had two girls with her?

John was shocked; how can a mother do that? That she chose her happiness over her own daughters'. He then divorced her, and that mother left to live a happy life, while the girls stayed with John.

John knew that things had gotten more difficult. How will he be able to pay for those girls?

That's why he was forced to work two jobs, in order to fill in the space his ex-wife had left.

He didn't see the girls much because he worked day and night for them. He worked even on weekends, part-time; with the time left, he would spend it with his girls, and he would take them out. He hired a nanny to stay with them, while he went to work. He never let the girls feel that anything was missing, for he would put them over his own health and his needs.

All of that stress he felt would fly away with the wind when he came back from work at midnight and saw his girls in deep sleep. One time, as he came home from work, he heard the two girls talking, and he stood behind the door to listen to them. Oh how he wished he hadn't done so.

He heard them talk about how embarrassed they would be when their dad came to school because of his funny look. Yes John didn't take care of his looks because he never found the time to do that, but those girls couldn't appreciate that.

That wasn't all he heard; one of the girls even said that she wished her friend's dad was her dad instead because he was wealthy and his style, and because he always bought her toys and took her around the world each year. The other one said that if their mother came back, their life would have been much better than this filthy life.

John had told them that their mother just traveled, and that she would come back. He always believed that his wife would come back because he loved her very much, and he thought it was a mistake, and that she would regret it and come back.

John listened to those words while he almost choked in pain. What more do these girls want? John is a human not a machine, and they weren't in need of anything. He was crying, and it's something very hard for a man to cry.

The mother who left her children was their hero, while the one who gave them everything was the one who brought them shame; that's what the two girls believed.

John did something very strange that no one else would do; he wrote letters to his ex-wife. Those letters expressed his feelings of pain, and how he still loved her and missed her despite everything, but he never sent those to her. There was an old building near his house; that building was abandoned completely, and no one worked there. John would creep in at night and place the letters in the broken mailbox. No one knows why he did that, or what the benefit of doing so is, but surely what he did made him feel better.

John didn't have true friends because he didn't talk to anyone, and if he did, he would talk about how much he loved his daughters. That's why people loved him, despite his non sociable lifestyle, whether with his neighbors or co-workers.

During the morning, he worked as a waiter at a high-end cafe. There was a young lady who regularly visited the place, and when you see her, you feel two things: that she is a successful business woman, or that she was the manager of an elite company. That woman only drank the coffee if John himself made it and brought it personally to her. Her eyes never looked away from him as he worked, and no one knew the reason behind that, or, in fact, no one dared to ask her.

That woman heard yelling coming from the employees' room; it was clear that there is a fight between the boss and one of the workers. The lady got up and left the cafe, and she walked around to the backdoor of the rear corner attached to the place. She found the boss and John yelling, and she listened closely. It was indicated that the boss was tired of John sleeping at work, and John was apologizing to him, telling him that it won't happen again, but his boss was saying that it wasn't the first time, and he reminded him that it was a place of work and not a hotel.

It was natural for John to fall asleep because he never slept at home. He begged him with all his power, as he thought of his kids. If he got fired, where would he get the money? A new job would need to put him under a test before he receives pay; that's why he begged, but his boss didn't care.

The woman was stunned when she saw John fall down to his knees, begging. She had goose bumps, for what degradation can come after that? He begged for his kids, but to no avail. His boss yelled for John to leave, and he left the place.

John was still on his knees, lost in thought; he had lost hope in everything. The lady finally approached him:

"There are many jobs out there, and you don't need to humiliate yourself anymore!"

She spoke in a strict tone, but she couldn't hide the tears that filled her eyes. John looked at her strangely as he got back up on his feet and replied:

"It's not prostration... When you have kids, you'll understand why I did that!"

He then left; what he meant by that is that he did what he did for his kids; to help myself believe that I did all I could to keep that job, but I won't regret the fact that I couldn't, in the future.

She looked at him and yelled:

"Wait!"

John stopped, until she approached him and took out a decent amount of money from her purse:

"Take this money."

He smiled at her and took the money; he then looked at the money while still smiling, then looked back at her:

"You're not going to be kinder than God on me."

He grabbed her hand, gave her the money back, and left, walking, to the unknown. The lady saw how upset he was, so she worried about him and decided to follow him.

She wasn't wrong in doing so because John was walking left and right; he looked like someone who had just walked out of a bar at mid-night. Thoughts filled his head. What will he do?

As he walked, the lady followed him. John suddenly stopped at a fast food place and found a man smoking cigarettes during his break; that man worked at the place.

John took out his wallet and found three dollars. Why did he do that? Because he promised his daughters that he would buy them two meals after school, but he doesn't have the money. He headed toward the man:

"Can you give me two meals, and I will clean the restaurant and give you three dollars on top."

The man was astonished as he saw the level of meltdown that appeared on John. He was a good guy, and he felt bad for John. While he looked, he was even more shocked when John fell down to his knees. No one knows why he did. Is it to beg, or because of his tiredness and mental condition had taken all his strength.

When the man saw that, he didn't hesitate. He lit off his cigarette:

"I'll go get the meals instantly. I want nothing in return!"

But John yelled:

"No... I'll clean and the three dollars or I won't take the meals."

The man stood and looked at John and his seriousness. He could do nothing but accept. He wasn't obliged but because of his humanitarian nature.

John entered there, and he began working and cleaning. Even though he was very tired and could barely stand up, but he promised his daughters.

The woman looked at John, but she didn't want him to notice her. He came out with the two meals, and the man had offered him money for his work because what he did deserved more than two meals, but John refused.

He headed for the house on foot; his steps were weakening, and his sight was blinded; tiredness overcame him, and he fell to the ground in the middle of the street as the food and drinks flew out of his hands.

People ran to him, including the lady, and she stopped a taxi as they carried him to the hospital. The doctors told her that he suffers from bad fatigue, and he needs to rest for a week's time.

Can you imagine what that news did to John? First, the hospital bill, then losing his job, and now resting for a week. If all of this happens, who will take care of his kids?

But that lady took care of all the bills. Not only that, but she also bought two meals from one of the fast food restaurants and took them to the girls, then she brought them to see their dad.

There is one important question: how did that lady know where John lived? Be sure that this lady knows everything about him. She has been watching him for years, and she spied on him and knew everything. Even that he went to that building to leave his letters. It was easy to know everything about John, whose moves were very predictable. Work, house, abandoned building-- that was his life in summary.

He woke up and found himself in the hospital, with his girls around him. There were many questions that he asked: Where am I? Who brought me here? How did the girls get here?

All of these questions could only be answered by that lady, who the girls told their dad about. He asked them to bring her to him, and to leave them alone.

That lady came and sat close by him; he was surprised to see his cafe customer, and she was called Jolie. He began asking her why she did all of that for him, and how she knew about his house and kids.

Her answer only told him that if something good happened, doesn't ask why.

John insisted on paying her back the treatment bill, and she didn't have a problem with it, as long as it made him happy.

Since that day, Jolie became the family friend. She visited them daily, and she would take the girls out and buy them presents. They were very happy, so was John. Gifts can't be given back, that's why he wasn't bothered when he saw Jolie getting them all those presents.

Everything seems to be going just fine for John. His girls have gotten older; one is thirteen, and the other one is eleven. That day, something strange happened. Their doorbell was ringing, and John went to see who it was. The surprise was his ex-wife. Without thinking, he quickly held her closer to him, despite everything, he still loved her, but he felt that hand, which extended and touched his chest, pushing him away, and she was wearing a wedding band also. She pushed him, and with a serious tone, she said:

"I am not here for you!"

John was surprised; he thought she had come back for them, but he was wrong:

"Then why are you here?"

She answered:

"Because of my daughters... I want to take them with me!"

John insanely laughed:

"The daughters you left behind when they needed you the most!"

She entered the house:

"They're the ones who will decide, not you!"

John angrily replied:

"You can't take them away even if they wanted to!"

She smiled in wickedness:

"Seems like I came to take them the easy way. You're forcing me to do something I don't want to do..."

John replied:

"I don't care what you say, whether it's the easy or hard way. You're not taking the girls!"

"You'll change your mind once you know the truth!" Was the reply to John's remark?

John asked:

"What truth?!"

She was silent for a moment before she answered:

"The truth is... These girls are not your daughters... You're sterile John!"

That shock was enough to send him two steps back:

"You're a liar! You're lying!"

She looked at him with a devil's eyes:

"Do the test, and they'll prove what I am telling you. Do you remember the night we went for a test? I told the doctor not to tell you the truth for the sake of your feelings. The father of those girls is my current husband. Your turn, which was to save me the trouble of rising the, is now over. They're older now, and I can take care of them.

She left him and called the two girls. They knew who she was because they had many pictures of her, so they were very pleased to see her. She told them that she was here to take them to live the life they deserve instead of this miserable life. They asked if their dad was coming, and she said no. They held their mother's hand and walked in front of John who watched as they left without saying a word. He was still astonished by the news he heard, which almost stopped his heart.

What John was witnessing took him back to the night his wife first left, only this time she took the girls, who turned out not be his own, and they left without even saying goodbye.

John went to a nearby clinic, and the tests proved what his wife had said, and that he was sterile since birth, not recently. He had a complete meltdown. He was putting all his weight against the wall as he walked. John has ended. All those years of sacrifice for the girls, who weren't even from the same blood, and they easily left him. His feet took him to the unknown as he could barely carry himself. He fell down about a thousand times before reaching the house. He entered the house and felt out of breath. There was nothing at his house but that fire place; he fell to the chair as tears flooded his eyes, and he couldn't breathe. John was taking his last breath.

Jolie, as usual, was coming to the house, not knowing what had taken place. She knocked the door, and no one answered, so she walked over to the window, and saw John on the chair dying. She ran quickly inside and began shake him as he cried and choked. She saw that paper he held, and she found out the truth, but she only heard the sound of that scary breath John was taking, as if his soul was leaving his body.

Jolie took him to the hospital. She was frightened and in tears. The doctor told her that he was in a coma, and that heart attack could cost his life, but they will do what they can, despite the thin line of hope. The machines were what kept him alive.

Jolie never left him; she would always visit him and see how he was doing, but the only thing left of John was his body.

Every time she visited him, she would talk about many things, and this time she wanted to talk about herself. She wanted to tell him these words before he went into the coma:

"Do you remember that old man that always accompanied me to the cafe you used to work at? He died, and I am now alone. He was the one who planted the love of that place in my heart. My dad loved me very much, despite his business with his work; he was never late for me. He would tell me that he had lost many deals because of me. If I called him, he would leave everything and come quickly, even during his important meetings. I used to tell him that I'll never find a man like him, but he would tell me that there are a lot of good people. I never believed that, but when I heard one of your co-workers talking to his friend about you, I was curious to know the person they talked about. Their words were great about a man who gave everything for his daughters. That reminded me of my father. I would pay them to give me information about you. I admired you very much until that fight took place at the cafe; it was the best chance. I was very happy when I became closer to you and your daughters. I won't hide the fact that I was in pain, and I am still in pain because you only saw me as a friend. Even though you became everything to me. I've lost security since my dad died, but I began to feel that same feeling when I am with you. My closeness to you hid the fact that I was just a friend. I love you John... I love you..."

Jolie cried as she told John her story, and she held his hand. Suddenly she felt the movement of his hand as if he wanted to hold hers. She looked at him and saw a tear coming down from his eye. It was like John had heard what she was saying; that fear turned into joy:

"John, you can hear me right?"

But he didn't answer, nor did he react in a way that indicated he could hear. She quickly went to the doctor and told him what happened, but he told her that it was normal for these things to happen to anyone in a coma. It's an unintentional reaction; the eyes fill with tears and shaking of the hands. All of these things do not indicate that John was getting better, or that he would wake up from the long coma.

Jolie never lost hope; she went to his ex-wife's house; after searching for her address, she was able to find the house. She wanted the girls to stand by John, but she was surprised to see that the girls were brainwashed by their mother, who filled their hearts with hatred. She received a response that she didn't expect; she told them that John wasn't their father, but that news weren't the only thing that changed their minds. They were already embarrassed by him, and they wished for another father, so they had gotten just that.

Jolie was surprised at how bitter they were. They forgot everything he had done for them, and they refused to go with her because John wasn't their dad, and there was nothing that connected them. If it's about what John has done then a thank you is enough.

Jolie knew that their mother had brainwashed them, and there was no way she could change their minds. She decided to stay with John until the end, and she wouldn't give up no matter what happens."

CHAPTER 11

THE OLD MAN

"There is one last thing I want you to see before I answer your questions. Be sure that you're closer than ever to receiving the answer to what you've endlessly asked yourselves and couldn't find any explanations. Now, everyone stand up please and follow me."

The old woman was in the front, and everyone was following her as if she was a tour guide, and the groups were the tourists. They weren't talking to each other; the reason may very well be that they were all thinking of what happened, and it may also be the thought of what will take place further on, therefore, talking wasn't the thought anyone was thinking.

Each time the old woman took a step forward, the fog would fade away, becoming like a roadway or alley, and vision would become clear from five or six meters away in each step she was taking.

They didn't walk much until the shadow of an abandoned house began to appear. It looked frightening; to the eyes of the one looking at it, it would seem like it's a cemetery instead of a house. The reason to that is not the design because the design was very modern, but it was mostly the absence of any source of light that made the house terrorizing. The sound of the formidable wind crossing in an out of openings in the house was the only thing the group heard; it was a house with no life.

Yes, everyone, without an exception, felt fearful on one hand and inquisition on the other, but the presence of the old woman eased their worries a little bit, for they know that she would never hurt them.

There was one question on everyone's mind as they thought to themselves:

"What is a house like this doing here? What kind of idiot thinks about walking hear, let alone building a house here!!?"

They all walked closer to it, but that short distance wasn't enough for them to make any details of the house, only the fact that it's a house.

When they closely approached that house, it became clearer because they were only a few steps away. It was made of fine would, with the color white specifically, and it appeared to be a two-story house. The roof was red, and the frontal exterior contained four windows; two in the lower part and two in the upper part; the door was built in the centermost part of it.

The thing that drew their attention was the lack of light inside and outside the house, despite all the windows being wide open.

The old woman headed toward the door, which opened without anyone forcing it to; she took a step inside and looked back at the group, who stood paralyzed; she ordered:

"Follow me inside."

They all did as she asked and walked into the frightening house; it was awfully dark to where they couldn't even see the old woman; when the last person walked in, the door and the windows closed shut, which sent chills within their souls. They all got closer to each other until they were almost glued to one another. They looked similar to a group of sheep fearing a wolf's attack.

Afterwards, the candles began to light up one after another in the shape of a square, making it easier to see. They found themselves in the living room; there wasn't any furniture, only the wooden floor. Is that truly all they saw?

No, because the old woman stood in the middle, but that wasn't the reason to their surprise. Behind her as an old man, over sixty years old; he had gray hair, and his face was deathly pale. It has turned into a strange white and blue color, similar to a corpse that has been in the water for some time. He was sitting on a chair as he looked at something very important; his eyes didn't even blink; his eyes saw everything around, but he seemed to not care.

What's that thing?

Alright, that old man was staring at a woman and another man who sat in front of him. They were both looking at the ground as if they didn't want to see anything else besides that floor underneath them.

The man appeared to be in his forties; he had short, black hair, and he was fair-skinned. On the right side of his head, there was a small hole. It was obvious, by the way it looked, that it was a bullet hole.

The woman was blonde, and her whole body was burned, therefore, it wasn't clear whether she was fair-skinned or not. The fire seemed to have eaten up her entire body, and it obliterated her features with the exception of her hair.

The old woman was looking at all who were present, and she saw in their eyes how shocked they were to witness such scene; she began to talk as she pointed her left hand toward the old man:

"I know that you haven't met before, but this man was supposed to be a part of your group. Unfortunately, he died; therefore, he wasn't a part of it. Of course there is a reason for that, and you'll know that later."

Even though they were all listening to her speak with their ears, their eyes were still watching the other three. What surprised them more was that the old man was still staring at the two, and his eyes have still not blinked, bur more extraordinarily was that the three didn't appear to notice the group's arrival because they hadn't looked at them, nor spoke a single word. It was as if the three were alone in that house.

The old woman continued:

"His name is Tom; he got married at twenty-five to the woman he had long loved with all his heart, and her name was Angelina. I can describe Tom's life in three words: wonderful... very wonderful.

How can it not be when he lives under one roof with the woman he loves? Angelina, in return, crazily adored him. As time passed, Angelina had a girl and a boy to complete the happiness in that house. Especially with the fact that children are the angels of every house, and they're the source of happiness in this life.

Death is the enemy of happiness. The death that doesn't know young or old, nor does it have mercy, but just likes he takes away, God gives back. God gave us the ability to forget and be patience.

When the boy turned 17, and the girl turned 10, illness was eating up Angelina's body; she became bedridden. Those are the last minutes for her in this life; it's the day that will never be wiped from Tom's memory. The kids were at school, and he was sitting with Angelina as she took her last grasps of air. Tom was crying as he stood helpless, watching the love of his life being taken from his hands. She raised her hand and wiped away his tears, saying:

"I hate seeing your tears. If I am leaving, the last thing I want to see is your smile."

She smiled as Tom held her hands, the hand that wiped away his tears; he held it with all his strength, and he began embracing them without saying a single word because words are useless in times like these.

Angelina looked at him and asked:

"Do you promise to do what I am going to ask you?"

If Tom had granted all her wishes without any problems, how can he not when it's her death wish?

He quickly replied:

"Of course my dear, anything you want!"

"Thank you," said Angelina, "The kids... The kids... Don't ever leave them, neither in weal, nor woe."

Those were the last words Angelina had spoken before departing this world, leaving Tom and his kids alone in this life.

Tom was deeply affected by the death of his wife. He cried like a little child. No matter how much we cry, the tears we shed won't be able to bring back those who have passed.

The only thing behind Tom's patience and resistance was Angelina's wish and the kids.

Tom honored his promise; he became the father, the mother, and the friend to his children to the extent where he almost made them forget their mother.

The years passed and the kids grew up and got married, only to bring back loneliness into Tom's heart. The house became quiet; he found himself abandoned. Memories filled his mind.

That emptiness wasn't because his kids got married because since their marriage, they completely deserted him. It's almost as if his kids never existed. Despite Tom's tries to call or visit them, they always avoided him. Tom felt that he was unwanted by his own kids, and he respected their desire. Although, he always asked himself why his kids did that to him.

Tom became a grandfather, and he now has grandchildren, but he found out by coincidence because his kids never informed him. He figured everything out on his own because he was still keeping his promise, and he always watched them from afar. Their maids always answered and told him that his kids weren't home.

One day he stood outside his son's house and saw him walking in; he called the house phone, but the maid was like a parrot, repeating the same sentence that he had heard for years: "He is not here."

Tom lost hope in them, therefore, he decided to stop calling them or getting close to them, but he continued watching them from a distance, and placing money into their banking accounts.

The son and daughter were competing to see who can avoid and abandon their father more.

Did life busy them? Did life take their time away? Can they not handle taking care of an old man?

When parents have their kids, they take care of them with everything they have, so that when they grow up, their kids would take care of them the same way their parents took care of them when they were younger. That never happened.

When Tom felt lonely, he went to whom he had felt comfort with; the woman who had taken care of him--Angelina.

He went to her grave and sat close to it; he began:

"Did you know that this would happen? I am sure you had known. My kids have left me, my love."

A tear fell from his eye, and how he wished that gentle hand would raise up and wipe that tear away, but she is gone.

He continued:

"I've done all I can do, but I've become an outcast. Do you know what that means? But I've decided to leave them alone, but my eyes will remain open, and I will always be there if they need me. I love you Angelina; you don't know how much I've missed you.

Tom secluded himself from everything afterwards, and he stayed in his house. Every occasion, he would wait near the phone, whether it was his birthday or any other occasion, for he had never lost hope in them, but he soon would succumb to the truth; he is still unwanted. Tom knew that if it weren't for the money he sends to his kids, they would be completely lost. Especially his son, who loved money. He always bet on stocks and lost, but his dad's money always helped him when he was in need.

Years passed like lightning; one day it was Tom's birthday. As usual, he waited near the phone and looked at the clock; it was 12:05, and no one called. He started to remember those beautiful days when everyone would gather, and Angelina was alive. When his kids were young, and how the atmosphere was astonishing and beautiful; everyone competed to see who would blow the candles off first. Now, the one thing turning those candles off is his tears.

Every occasion was mourning for Tom, and he suffered awfully much from them. These occasions became what he dreaded the most, and he wished that it would be deleted from the calendar.

It's 12:15 a.m. -- fifteen minutes after the time of his birthday. Tom started to feel suffocated, he felt a bitter coldness. Everything around him spun around, and his movement became heavy. He felt as if everything was disappearing-- it was a heart attack.

Tom gathered all his strength to head toward the phone to use it. He succeeded, and after a difficulty, he grabbed the phone. It was instinct and easiest for him to call the ambulance, but his hands were functioning through a signal from his heart and not his brain, and they dialed. It was his son's number. He wished to hear his son's voice and wanted it to be the last thing he hears, but when he tried to dial the last number, he passed away."

The old lady stopped talking; as soon as she had done so, Tom's soul disappeared in front of everyone. A strong wind blew after the windows suddenly swung open; the candles swayed along. With that, the wind took Tom's soul from this place. The wind suddenly stopped after his soul disappeared, and the windows were closed shut again.

Everyone was in a state of amazement and terror because everything happened quickly. They all turned their eyes toward the old lady to see what she had to say. She continued, saying:

"No one mourned his death except for a few people. The ones who were able to see him after his seclusion from the outside world. The moment for remembrance in honor of Tom. There were many people in line to talk about this great man: the neighbors and his old friends. As for his own kids, they wished that this line would never end, and they wished not to be there.

People came up to the podium and began talking about everything beautiful in that man. The time that his son was dreading came; it was his turn to speak. He was shivering as he stood behind the podium. His face was as pale as that of a deceased person's, not because of his father's death, for that incident hadn't affected neither him nor his sister, but it's the fear of what he was going to say. Especially to his own kids, who didn't even now they had a grandfather, which made things much worse? It seemed as if had distinctly heard his father's voice say:

"What are you waiting for my son...? Tell them the truth... The truth my son."

The son froze in his place due to his fearfulness. The guests began whispering amongst each other; why doesn't he speak?

The same voice was still circling within his mind:

"Tell your sons that I had unsuccessfully tried to get closer to you, but both you and your sister always avoided me."

The son suddenly yelled:

"Stop!"

The guests were all surprised about what happened; has he lost his mind?

He buried his head into his hands as if to gather his strength; he finally spoke, and it would have been much better if he had remained quiet--that's what everyone thought to themselves. The son, looking at his kids, said:

"My children, do you remember those beautiful presents that you received during any occasion? They weren't from me or your mother; they're from that man... Your grandfather!"

He finished, pointing at his father's grave.

His sister took that chance and escaped while everyone's attention was directed at her brother, who didn't add another word, and he left the place.

Tom was buried alone without the presence of his kids, who both left. Tom has now gone to the woman he loved."

The old lady stopped talking for a minute, and she turned around to look at the man and woman standing behind her. She stared at them for a good amount of time; she then looked back at the group and said as she pointed at the man:

"Do you see this man? He loved money more than himself, and if you love money this much, you won't be able to leave it. This man devoted his whole life to collecting money, not taking into account anything else. When the economy crisis took place, everyone lost their money. He couldn't handle the shock, so he shot himself, taking his own life. "

She then looked at the woman, pointed at her, and continued:

"That woman loved her kids greatly. One day, their house lit up in flames, and she put her life on the lines to save her kids. She was able to do so, but you can see what that cost her. She is completely distorted. Her children were supposed to owe her their lives, but instead, they ran away from her because of her face. Her terrifying appearance made them cry and flee to their father. They didn't want her to touch them or even see them. She didn't live very long; she died later due to the pain of her burns, and the anguish from what her kids had done."

The old woman turned to the group again and asked:

"Do you know who those two are?"

No one answered, so she continued:

"They're Tom's kids! They tasted the same bitterness they gave to their father. The son who left his dad for money. Money was his murderer. As for the daughter, she understood the meaning of what she had done, and she felt that fire that was burning in her dad's heart."

When the old woman finished, the same exact thing that had happened to Tom took place. The windows opened, and the wind blew quickly and too the two souls, leaving the house.

Silence hovered over the place, but the old woman broke that silence boundary:

"I hope you've learned from this lesson, but what's the meaning of it? It's the last moment. We're on our away to answer that question: why is this happening to me? Now follow me." She ordered.

She left the house, and everyone followed her. Fog was still covering that place. When they took a few steps, the house disappeared as if it was never there.

Yes, everyone was thinking of Tom's story, but there was something more important to think about--them and what's waiting for them what's the answer to that question they had long asked?

CHAPTER 12

THE TRUTH

What's the atmosphere after all of these stories?

Surely it wasn't a content one; when you hear the thing that hurts you the most, of course, it's going to be sad. Some of them buried their heads between their hands, while some chewed on their fingernails. Others closed their eyes, and the rest lowered their heads, looking at the ground.

The old lady looked at each of them, while they were suffering, and she began talking:

"I am sorry... It's something painful, I know. Some of you were surprised I told you some things that you didn't know about yourselves. Also, some of your stories began at childhood, others in the middle, and the rest near the end of your lives. I also know that there are many questions you long to answer. There might be a question in a different way for you. From why did this happen to me to why do that happen to them? But all of these questions do not equal to the one question in each of your minds; why does that happen to us?

Of course you won't ask the question; you're now closer than ever to finding out the answer. I want you all to stand up and follow me now."

But it seems like John has another view, for he looked at the old woman and said:

"Hey old lady... Seems like you forgot something?"

She looked at him:

"And what's that John?"

"The man that disappeared into the fog... Who was he?"

She smiled at that question and answered:

"He is no one; you can say he is just an actor to make sure none of you leave this circle."

Tony quickly said:

"What makes you so sure that we won't leave now?"

She laughed loudly:

"Look at yourself and those around you... You're all dying to know the truth more than anything; now follow me!"

"There is one last thing I want you to see before I answer your questions. Be sure that you're closer than ever to receiving the answer to what you've endlessly asked yourselves and couldn't find any explanations. Now, everyone stand up please and follow me."

The old woman was in the front, and everyone was following her as if she was a tour guide, and the groups were the tourists. They weren't talking to each other; the reason may very well be that they were all thinking of what happened, and it may also be the thought of what will take place further on, therefore, talking wasn't the thought anyone was thinking.

Each time the old woman took a step forward, the fog would fade away, becoming like a roadway or alley, and vision would become clear from five or six meters away in each step she was taking.

They didn't walk much until the shadow of an abandoned house began to appear. It looked frightening; to the eyes of the one looking at it, it would seem like it's a cemetery instead of a house. The reason to that is not the design because the design was very modern, but it was mostly the absence of any source of light that made the house terrorizing. The sound of the formidable wind crossing in an out of openings in the house was the only thing the group heard; it was a house with no life.

Yes, everyone, without an exception, felt fearful on one hand and inquisition on the other, but the presence of the old woman eased their worries a little bit, for they know that she would never hurt them.

There was one question on everyone's mind as they thought to themselves:

"What is a house like this doing here? What kind of idiot thinks about walking hear, let alone building a house here!!?"

They all walked closer to it, but that short distance wasn't enough for them to make any details of the house, only the fact that it's a house.

When they closely approached that house, it became clearer because they were only a few steps away. It was made of fine would, with the color white specifically, and it appeared to be a two-story house. The roof was red, and the frontal exterior contained four windows; two in the lower part and two in the upper part; the door was built in the centermost part of it.

The thing that drew their attention was the lack of light inside and outside the house, despite all the windows being wide open.

The old woman headed toward the door, which opened without anyone forcing it to; she took a step inside and looked back at the group, who stood paralyzed; she ordered:

"Follow me inside."

They all did as she asked and walked into the frightening house; it was awfully dark to where they couldn't even see the old woman; when the last person walked in, the door and the windows closed shut, which sent chills within their souls. They all got closer to each other until they were almost glued to one another. They looked similar to a group of sheep fearing a wolf's attack.

Afterwards, the candles began to light up one after another in the shape of a square, making it easier to see. They found themselves in the living room; there wasn't any furniture, only the wooden floor. Is that truly all they saw?

No, because the old woman stood in the middle, but that wasn't the reason to their surprise. Behind her as an old man, over sixty years old; he had gray hair, and his face was deathly pale. It has turned into a strange white and blue color, similar to a corpse that has been in the water for some time. He was sitting on a chair as he looked at something very important; his eyes didn't even blink; his eyes saw everything around, but he seemed to not care.

What's that thing?

Alright, that old man was staring at a woman and another man who sat in front of him. They were both looking at the ground as if they didn't want to see anything else besides that floor underneath them.

The man appeared to be in his forties; he had short, black hair, and he was fair-skinned. On the right side of his head, there was a small hole. It was obvious, by the way it looked, that it was a bullet hole.

The woman was blonde, and her whole body was burned, therefore, it wasn't clear whether she was fair-skinned or not. The fire seemed to have eaten up her entire body, and it obliterated her features with the exception of her hair.

The old woman was looking at all who were present, and she saw in their eyes how shocked they were to witness such scene; she began to talk as she pointed her left hand toward the old man:

"I know that you haven't met before, but this man was supposed to be a part of your group. Unfortunately, he died; therefore, he wasn't a part of it. Of course there is a reason for that, and you'll know that later."

Even though they were all listening to her speak with their ears, their eyes were still watching the other three. What surprised them more was that the old man was still staring at the two, and his eyes have still not blinked, bur more extraordinarily was that the three didn't appear to notice the group's arrival because they hadn't looked at them, nor spoke a single word. It was as if the three were alone in that house.

The old woman continued:

"His name is Tom; he got married at twenty-five to the woman he had long loved with all his heart, and her name was Angelina. I can describe Tom's life in three words: wonderful... very wonderful.

How can it not be when he lives under one roof with the woman he loves? Angelina, in return, crazily adored him. As time passed, Angelina had a girl and a boy to complete the happiness in that house. Especially with the fact that children are the angels of every house, and they're the source of happiness in this life.

Death is the enemy of happiness. The death that doesn't know young or old, nor does it have mercy, but just likes he takes away, God gives back. God gave us the ability to forget and be patience.

When the boy turned 17, and the girl turned 10, illness was eating up Angelina's body; she became bedridden. Those are the last minutes for her in this life; it's the day that will never be wiped from Tom's memory. The kids were at school, and he was sitting with Angelina as she took her last grasps of air. Tom was crying as he stood helpless, watching the love of his life being taken from his hands. She raised her hand and wiped away his tears, saying:

"I hate seeing your tears. If I am leaving, the last thing I want to see is your smile."

She smiled as Tom held her hands, the hand that wiped away his tears; he held it with all his strength, and he began embracing them without saying a single word because words are useless in times like these.

Angelina looked at him and asked:

"Do you promise to do what I am going to ask you?"

If Tom had granted all her wishes without any problems, how can he not when it's her death wish?

He quickly replied:

"Of course my dear, anything you want!"

"Thank you," said Angelina, "The kids... The kids... Don't ever leave them, neither in weal, nor woe."

Those were the last words Angelina had spoken before departing this world, leaving Tom and his kids alone in this life.

Tom was deeply affected by the death of his wife. He cried like a little child. No matter how much we cry, the tears we shed won't be able to bring back those who have passed.

The only thing behind Tom's patience and resistance was Angelina's wish and the kids.

Tom honored his promise; he became the father, the mother, and the friend to his children to the extent where he almost made them forget their mother.

The years passed and the kids grew up and got married, only to bring back loneliness into Tom's heart. The house became quiet; he found himself abandoned. Memories filled his mind.

That emptiness wasn't because his kids got married because since their marriage, they completely deserted him. It's almost as if his kids never existed. Despite Tom's tries to call or visit them, they always avoided him. Tom felt that he was unwanted by his own kids, and he respected their desire. Although, he always asked himself why his kids did that to him.

Tom became a grandfather, and he now has grandchildren, but he found out by coincidence because his kids never informed him. He figured everything out on his own because he was still keeping his promise, and he always watched them from afar. Their maids always answered and told him that his kids weren't home.

One day he stood outside his son's house and saw him walking in; he called the house phone, but the maid was like a parrot, repeating the same sentence that he had heard for years: "He is not here."

Tom lost hope in them, therefore, he decided to stop calling them or getting close to them, but he continued watching them from a distance, and placing money into their banking accounts.

The son and daughter were competing to see who can avoid and abandon their father more.

Did life busy them? Did life take their time away? Can they not handle taking care of an old man?

When parents have their kids, they take care of them with everything they have, so that when they grow up, their kids would take care of them the same way their parents took care of them when they were younger. That never happened.

When Tom felt lonely, he went to whom he had felt comfort with; the woman who had taken care of him-- Angelina.

He went to her grave and sat close to it; he began:

"Did you know that this would happen? I am sure you had known. My kids have left me, my love."

A tear fell from his eye, and how he wished that gentle hand would raise up and wipe that tear away, but she is gone.

He continued:

"I've done all I can do, but I've become an outcast. Do you know what that means? But I've decided to leave them alone, but my eyes will remain open, and I will always be there if they need me. I love you Angelina; you don't know how much I've missed you.

Tom secluded himself from everything afterwards, and he stayed in his house. Every occasion, he would wait near the phone, whether it was his birthday or any other occasion, for he had never lost hope in them, but he soon would succumb to the truth; he is still unwanted. Tom knew that if it weren't for the money he sends to his kids, they would be completely lost. Especially his son, who loved money. He always bet on stocks and lost, but his dad's money always helped him when he was in need.

Years passed like lightning; one day it was Tom's birthday. As usual, he waited near the phone and looked at the clock; it was 12:05, and no one called. He started to remember those beautiful days when everyone would gather, and Angelina was alive. When his kids were young, and how the atmosphere was astonishing and beautiful; everyone competed to see who would blow the candles off first. Now, the one thing turning those candles off is his tears.

Every occasion was mourning for Tom, and he suffered awfully much from them. These occasions became what he dreaded the most, and he wished that it would be deleted from the calendar.

It's 12:15 a.m. -- fifteen minutes after the time of his birthday. Tom started to feel suffocated, he felt a bitter coldness. Everything around him spun around, and his movement became heavy. He felt as if everything was disappearing-- it was a heart attack.

Tom gathered all his strength to head toward the phone to use it. He succeeded, and after a difficulty, he grabbed the phone. It was instinct and easiest for him to call the ambulance, but his hands were functioning through a signal from his heart and not his brain, and they dialed. It was his son's number. He wished to hear his son's voice and wanted it to be the last thing he hears, but when he tried to dial the last number, he passed away. "

The old lady stopped talking; as soon as she had done so, Tom's soul disappeared in front of everyone. A strong wind blew after the windows suddenly swung open; the candles swayed along. With that, the wind took Tom's soul from this place. The wind suddenly stopped after his soul disappeared, and the windows were closed shut again.

Everyone was in a state of amazement and terror because everything happened quickly. They all turned their eyes toward the old lady to see what she had to say. She continued, saying:

"No one mourned his death except for a few people. The ones who were able to see him after his seclusion from the outside world. The moment for remembrance in honor of Tom. There were many people in line to talk about this great man: the neighbors and his old friends. As for his own kids, they wished that this line would never end, and they wished not to be there.

People came up to the podium and began talking about everything beautiful in that man. The time that his son was dreading came; it was his turn to speak. He was shivering as he stood behind the podium. His face was as pale as that of a deceased person's, not because of his father's death, for that incident hadn't affected neither him nor his sister, but it's the fear of what he was going to say. Especially to his own kids, who didn't even now they had a grandfather, which made things much worse. It seemed as if had distinctly heard his father's voice say:

107

"What are you waiting for my son.. Tell them the truth... The truth my son."

The son froze in his place due to his fearfulness. The guests began whispering amongst each other; why doesn't he speak?

The same voice was still circling within his mind:

"Tell your sons that I had unsuccessfully tried to get closer to you, but both you and your sister always avoided me."

The son suddenly yelled:

"Stop!"

The guests were all surprised about what happened; has he lost his mind?

He buried his head into his hands as if to gather his strength; he finally spoke, and it would have been much better if he had remained quiet--that's what everyone thought to themselves. The son, looking at his kids, said:

"My children, do you remember those beautiful presents that you received during any occasion? They weren't from me or your mother; they're from that man.. Your grandfather!"

He finished, pointing at his father's grave.

His sister took that chance and escaped while everyone's attention was directed at her brother, who didn't add another word, and he left the place.

Tom was buried alone without the presence of his kids, who both left. Tom has now gone to the woman he loved."

The old lady stopped talking for a minute, and she turned around to look at the man and woman standing behind her. She stared at them for a good amount of time; she then looked back at the group and said as she pointed at the man:

"Do you see this man? He loved money more than himself, and if you love money this much, you won't be able to leave it. This man devoted his whole life to collecting money, not taking into account anything else. When the economy crisis took place, everyone lost their money. He couldn't handle the shock, so he shot himself, taking his own life. "

She then looked at the woman, pointed at her, and continued:

"That woman loved her kids greatly. One day, their house lit up in flames, and she put her life on the lines to save her kids. She was able to do so, but you can see what that cost her. She is completely distorted. Her children were supposed to owe her their lives, but instead, they ran away from her because of her face. Her terrifying appearance made them cry and flee to their father. They didn't want her to touch them or even see them. She didn't live very long; she died later due to the pain of her burns, and the anguish from what her kids had done."

The old woman turned to the group again and asked:

"Do you know who those two are?"

No one answered, so she continued:

"They're Tom's kids! They tasted the same bitterness they gave to their father. The son who left his dad for money. Money was his murderer. As for the daughter, she understood the meaning of what she had done, and she felt that fire that was burning in her dad's heart."

When the old woman finished, the same exact thing that had happened to Tom took place. The windows opened, and the wind blew quickly and too the two souls, leaving the house.

Silence hovered over the place, but the old woman broke that silence boundary:

"I hope you've learned from this lesson,but what's the meaning of it? It's the last moment. We're on our away to answer that question: why is this happening to me? Now follow me." She ordered.

She left the house, and everyone followed her. Fog was still covering that place. When they took a few steps, the house disappeared as if it was never there.

Yes, everyone was thinking of Tom's story, but there was something more important to think about--themselves and what's waiting for them What's the answer to that question they had long asked?

Fog was still surrounding the outskirts of that house. The old woman walked in the front while everyone else followed. Each path she took the fog would vanish while she walked. She walked for five minutes, and they couldn't do anything but follow without saying a word. It wasn't a short distance, so it was natural for them to start talking to each other; especially Tony and Samantha, and Jessica and Martin.

Tony, who was walking by Samantha, came closer to her and began:

"I am sorry about what happened."

She smiled:

"Thanks!"

But Tony quickly reacted:

"No, what I am saying is not just because I feel bad. That store that Michael took you to is actually mine. He came to me one day asking for it, and I didn't have a problem with it, but I didn't know he wanted it for you."

Samantha gave him a strange look, but she didn't answer him. She turned around and continued walking because she thought that what he said didn't deserve an answer, but Tony didn't stop:

"Michael is not the bad person you think he is! He is my close friend, and I know him very well. He suffered in his childhood; his father left him at a young age, and his mother treated him horribly. Each day she had a new lover; he would see his mom coming to the house with a different guy everyday. That's why women became an issue in his life, and he was seeking revenge on all of them. He lies to them and hurts them and that's what made him feel better."

Samantha suddenly stopped and looked at him:

"Why are you telling me this?"

He looked back at her:

"Because I was shocked when I heard the old woman say that he actually admitted he didn't love you. Michael never did that; he only left them in wonder. Also those looks in his eyes when he wanted the store from me; he loves you Samantha. I am very sure and I know Michael well.

Martin walked closer to Jessica, and offered his condolences:

"I am sorry about what happened to William."

She turned to him with a bright smile:

"Thank you. I used to think that William was the only one who sacrificed everything for his family, but when I heard your story and John's story, I understood that there are still some good people, and that there is more than one person like William."

They exchanged smiles and walked side by side.

The old woman suddenly stopped and turned around to look at them:

"I want you all to stand in a straight line, close to each other, and I want you to close your eyes. Don't open them for any reason, and when I say for any reason, I mean it."

They all did what she asked because they knew she was serious and not joking. All of them stood in a straight line, nearby each other.

John, Tony, Samantha, Madison, Katherine, Kevin, Martin, and Jessica-- that was the order in which they stood from left to right. They closed their eyes and began waiting for what will happen. They were scared, of course, but they've reached the end; there is no turning back. They're about to find out the answer to the question, which they were ready to give up their lives for.

Why is this happening to me?

The fog completely vanished until a large volcano stood fifty meters away. Snow was covering those mountains, but they couldn't see that since their eyes were closed.

Suddenly, everyone felt an earthquake; the ground was vigorously shaking beneath their feet. Their hearts began beating faster. The volcano erupted all of a sudden, and balls of fire flew out heading towards them. The snow began melting from the heat as well

The old woman yelled, reminding them:

"Don't open your eyes!"

That erupted volcano was throwing the balls of fire around them; when it came closer, everyone began hearing terrifying cries within each ball, coming their way. Their eyes were still closed. Within each ball, there were people screaming and crying. Their cries gave goose bumps to everyone who was present. Those blood curling screams were those of the humans suffering from the bad incidents, taking place in their lives. Some of them have lost their lovers; others suffered from the brutality of life. The group had the slightest clue on what was going on around them; all they heard were those terrorizing cries that said:

"Why? Why is this happening to me?"

Their wails were frightening, and everyone was horrified. Some of them covered their ears to block the noise out; Martin held Jessica's hand and told her not to be afraid because he was there. Their reactions differed, but none dared to open their eyes. They sensed the eruption and the collisions of the fire balls beside them, but they knew not to mess with the old lady and open their eyes. Even though no one would blame them if they did.

Suddenly the woman ordered:

"Open your eyes!"

Everyone opened their eyes and found the fire balls only half a meter away from each of them. They all stepped back, without an exception. If you open your eyes and see a fire ball in front of you, it's something terrifying, but they were also surprised that they couldn't feel the heat despite the fire surrounding them.

Those fire balls were circular and kind of flat; within, each contained a glass surface, similar to a TV, or the crystal balls that witches used to see things, which also resembles the ones in cartoons.

The old lady finally spoke:

"Don't worry, it won't burn you. All I want from you is to focus on the center; inside, you will see the fate you would've chosen yourself. What you will see is real and not an illusion. You can say it's a test to see how much you'll sacrifice for the benefit of others. Is it similar to the one they made for you or more? Less? Maybe even none. Now focus your eyes on those fireballs."

In the center of that ball, their chosen fates appeared. As for John, he saw that night that he was fighting with his wife. The fight got very big that he asked her to take the girls with her, so she takes them with her and throws them at a shelter. John saw the two girls crying at that shelter calling his name and their mother's name. They were frightened. Each night they would sit at the shelter's doorsteps waiting for their parents, but they still believe in him. One was crying, while the other was consoling her by telling her they were coming back. John's hand went up trying to reach in that ball, but it suddenly turned off and disappeared. The old woman approached him and whispered into his ear:

"Did you see the fate you chose? God chose for you to raise them up because he knew that their mother was going to leave them at an orphanage, to live the life of orphans, even though their parents were alive. You were born sterile, but since he loved you and was proud of you, he helped you feel the fatherhood. You've done an outstanding job handling that test from God, and you've passed. Even if they're not your kids, let me tell you that there is still hope, so don't lose hope in God. You never know what he has in store of you."

Tony saw that after Kate was diagnosed with cancer, she became very lonely, and she would always cry. He tried to stand by her, but she suffered a lot because she wasn't like all the other girls. She felt much pain while hiding the truth behind that wig. He saw that he had ran out of patience because of that miserable life, and he divorced her. After she had given everything for him, so she committed suicide because there was no reason for her to say alive now. Tony also reached out into the ball, but it,too, vanished into thin air.

The old lady came to him and said:

"Did you see that Tony? You weren't wrong for making her undergo treatment. You thought that you did so because you loved her, but you showed much more selfishness than love. All you think about is being with her, not caring about the amount of pain she will go through. You didn't understand her looks when she told you that she will sacrifice for you, even though she was sure you would leave her in the end."

Samantha saw that her friend Sara came and told her the truth about Michael and that Sara found out he was playing with her emotions. Samantha goes to Michael and faces him with the truth, and he wanted to explain to her, but she didn't give him a chance. He followed her, begging her to stop, but she refused. Michael then goes to a tall building near the park, and he throws himself from the top of that high building. His eyes were full of tears as if he had lost everything that moment, and nothing was worthy of living for.

Samantha was also approached by the old woman:

"Michael lied to you in what he said that night. Sara had found out about his past because one of her friends was a victim of his. Tony also told you the truth; Sara went to Michael and told him to leave you, but not without a warning. She threatened that if he didn't do exactly that, she would tell you everything. He didn't want to do that because he loved you, but his past is an obstacle between the both of you. He wanted to open a new page with you because it was the first time he had felt the true meaning of love with you. His words hinted to the presence of a new woman in his life, and you saw Sara with him that night, thinking that she is the woman he loved. The truth is: that night he asked to see her just to ask how you were doing, and she was not the woman he told you about, for that woman does not even exist in his life. He only did that for you, even though he would lose you either ways, but he preferred lying to you than telling you his past. He succeeded, but everyone makes mistakes. He still hopes that you'd go back to him, despite everything. If you don't, he will commit suicide no doubt."

Madison witnessed that she became more and more famous each day, until she became egotistic; she began looking down on the people around her. Then she was telling them that she is the reason they're famous, and that they're nothing but trash who live that good life because of her.

She saw how much her words were hurting the, and how ashamed and embarrassed they were; not only that, but she also kicked them all out of the band and took off singing by herself, while the other band members attended her concerts with eyes full of revenge, but she couldn't care less.

The old woman walked closer to Madison and whispered:

"Do you know what mostly hurts the people that work under a leader? When they learn that their leader has transformed from a heroine to a villain. When that view shakes in their eyes, and their leader is nothing but an illusion; it's very difficult. You became the prey; you entered the world of drugs, the prison, and the rehabilitation center just to feel exactly what they would have felt. They left you now because you gave up completely, and you didn't want to help yourself. You became a prisoner at that center, but be sure that they still believe in you, only if you believe in yourself again."

Katherine watched how her grandmother never forbade her from interacting with her uncle and his kids, and she told her the truth. Katherine then began hearing a lot of painful words from them, which planted hatred in her heart because she was still very young, so she began planting bad thoughts into her into her grandmother's head, until she started developing hatred toward her son. The grandmother then granted full ownership of everything she had to Katherine, and when she suddenly died, Katherine didn't give her uncle any shares. Not only that, but his house also belonged to his mother, so the day of revenge came, and she kicked him out of the house along with his family without any mercy.

The old woman came and whispered to Katherine:

"That is the fate you would have chosen. You're seeking revenge on the family that took you in when you're an orphan, and they gave you everything. God also knew that Jacqueline's death would leave a huge, empty space in her mother's life, since her son doesn't care for her. That's why he made Jacqueline choose you from all the children to take care of her mother until she died and to make her feel as if Jacqueline was still alive in you."

Kevin saw that Diana didn't die, and she gave birth to his son, so because of that, he ignored his mother. He didn't care for her anymore because of her old age; he also saw that he sent her to the nursing home because she could find the missing care there. He then saw his mother sitting in a wheelchair and her non-stop tears, while she stayed at that nursing home. When it would be visiting times, she would push that wheel with all her strength, and her hands that almost burned because of that pushing. She would search for Kevin, but since he sent her there, he never came back, once, to visit her. She never lost hope, but she did the same thing every time, hoping he would come to her, but she would go back slowly pushing that wheel; she was hurt and heartbroken. Kevin was very much able to see the difference of when the visiting time starts, and how happy she would be. Then he would see how she went back in the end --sad and destroyed.

The old woman came closer to Kevin and whispered:

"You see that fate that you wanted? But God wanted you to feel him, and your best friend David. He wanted you to feel the amount of pain you would have caused on your mother."

Martin saw himself as a teenager, and he left his dad's house and left him alone with his wife. He cut any connection between him and his father, so his wife took everything from him and left him also. His father goes to look for his son, and he found him. Martin kicked him out and shut the door in his face. The father then begins to talk after he lost everything: his wife, his son, and his house. He then falls down to the ground from a heart attack, and there wasn't anyone around to help him, so he dies alone with no one caring for him.

She walked closer to Martin and whispered to him:

"That's the fate you would have chosen. When your father abused you, be sure that he saw himself in you. He didn't have the courage to face the truth of his weakness.

He would abuse you monstrously as if he was doing it to himself. God gave you patience to stand by your father's side when he needed you the most. You weren't wrong about that drawing because your father loved you. That's why he didn't want you to leave the house or leave school."

Jessica saw that William never went to Iraq, because of her. He stayed at the farm answering her demand. When she turned eighteen, William bought her a car. The first day she drove, she got in an accident due to her reckless driving. Not only that, but she was also drunk. She had celebrated the day of getting her license by getting too drunk and driving. She then caused that tragic accident, which led to the death of three people: a mother, a father, and their child. Jessica then called William, who came running like a person who had just their mind, and he saw how scared she was, so he decided to take responsibility. He sacrificed for her and claimed that he was the one driving at the time of the accident. She didn't mind at all because she thought that him going to jail is better than her. He was tried and put in jail for a long time, which caused the massive collapse of their family, and they sold their farm because money wasn't available, and their son was in prison.

The old lady took a few steps toward Jessica and whispered:

"What William did for you made you lose the concept of responsibility. You didn't appreciate what he did for you. That's why God made him go to Iraq, so that he wouldn't be the victim of your mistakes. Also for you to understand and appreciate the amount of giving and sacrifice he had done for you."

She then took a few steps back, while everyone was still shocked because of what they'd just seen in that ball of fire; she began talking:

"Now you can choose between two fates; the fate you've chosen, or the one God had chosen for you. If you choose your fate, you will go back to the time before everything happened, and your memory will be gone. The same exact thing that you've all just witnessed would happen. If you choose God's fate, you will go back to the situation before I came, and this occurrence will remain in your memory. It may even be a reason to continue your lives. When you choose, each of you will go to the fate you've chosen, and I am sure you will choose what's best for you. My part has ended; I loved you all since the first time I met you. I want to tell you something: you are not bad people like you may think you are, because if you were, God wouldn't have put you through that difficult test. He believed in you the same way you've all believed in him. Now I must go, and remember to make the right choice.

She turned her back to leave, but she heard Kevin ask: "Who are you?"

Kevin seems like he's fully sane, but he is in the best condition ever. She didn't look at him, but she smiled. Suddenly she turned into a strange creature, with light shining from it. It had wings, and it spread them. It looked amazing. It was the most wonderful thing they'd ever seen. It was angel, but neither a female, nor male; it was just an angel, and it said:

"I am a messenger from God."

It then flew to the sky, until no one can see it.

Suddenly, it was like a hand reached out and pulled each of them strongly and lighting speed. All of them went back to the place where the messenger met them. What had happened was nothing but a dream, but not for them because what they saw was real and not just a dream. Something important had taken place: everyone's return to the place that creature had descended to them. That means one thing: all of them chose God's fate..

CHAPTER 13

THE ENDING

After they chose their fate, they had no idea of what will happen next. They're lost between two thoughts: assuming the best is yet to come, and that nothing could possibly be worse than what they had already endured.

Tony was at his house, and so was Samantha. John, Kevin, and Martin were in the hospital, while Madison was at the rehabilitation center, and Jessica was at the pond. Katherine was at one of the filthy alleys. It was morning , and the sun shone brightly announcing the beginning of a new day when each one of them woke up.

Tony found himself laying on kitchen floor; he began to look left and right, and he couldn't do anything but storm out of the house, lightening speed, to the hospital, where Kate was. He arrived there and headed towards her room, and the doctor had just came out. Tony approached him slowly and asked:

"How is Kate doing now?"

The doctor placed his gentle hand on Tony's shoulder as if to assure him that everything was going to be okay and replied with a sorrowfully voice:

"I am sorry... She has left.."

He looked at the doctor with complete disillusion; this shock was bigger than anything he can handle; it felt as if he had just received a final blow during a boxing match. His senseless body fell to the wall as he strongly buried his head between his two shaking hands and began crying; with tears flooding from his eyes,heartbroken, he mumbled:

"I wanted to see her.. I wanted to see her to apologize for being selfish... I am sorry Kate.. I am sorry." He continued crying.

The doctor came closer to him and tried everything he can to calm him down. Kate's departure was very painful for Tony, but it wasn't as agonizing as the pain he would have caused while letting her commit suicide.

At the funeral, everyone has come to say their last goodbyes to Kate, including Tony. He slowly approached her grave and gently placed a red rose; he said:

"It wasn't possible for me to see you before you left, but I am here today to tell you that I am very sorry for not understanding those looks in your eyes. I will cherish the sacrifices you made, Kate, and I know that you'll feel much happier when you're in God's hands because there, you don't have the need to cry everyday and to hide from people or be lonely and in solitude... I will miss you dearly, and I wish you a happy life there...." He concluded while wiping away what would not be the last of his tears and looked up to the sky.

Samantha woke up only to find herself in her bed. She looked around and found a white paper on her desk. She quickly headed towards it and opened it; she saw a drawing of the public park where she used to always go. There was a red dot before the hill that led to the bench where she usually sat. Without giving it much thought, nor having any doubts, she took off to the park to find out the meaning behind that red dot.

At the park, Samantha gave the drawing one last, brief look and continued in the direction of that dot. She found nothing but dirt with a few weeds, but when she tried to look closer, she saw that the dirt was uneven, for there was one strange bump that differed from the rest. She began to dig through until she felt something hard inside; she took it out and it seemed as if the thing was a piece of uncharted wood because of the dirt covering almost every inch of it. She began cleaning it gently until it became a bit clear. What Samantha saw made her eyes flood with tears because it was a piece of wood in the shape of a heart that was red in color, and in the middle, a wooden bench was carved with two people sitting on it. It wasn't difficult to determine that one was a female and the other was male because on top of the female was the name "Samantha" and "Michael" for the male, and above that bench were little hearts in resemblance to the stars at night. On the back, a note was written, saying:

"Happy birthday Samantha.. I love you." -Michael.

Her tears were falling down on the wood as she stood up to look at her surroundings; she was looking for Michael, but she couldn't find him. At that moment, she remembered the place she had seen Michael throw himself from; she gathered the strength to look towards the building, but she didn't find anything, despite it being very unclear to see on the roof of that building. She decided to head to the building and make sure he wasn't there.

Samantha arrived at the roof top, and as she caught her breath, she was shocked to see Michael, who looked like he was ready to throw himself off that building, but she yelled with all the strength she had left:

"WAIT!!"

That scream was loud enough to make him fall off whether he wanted to or not, but he didn't because that's the one thing he wanted to hear more than anything else at the time. He turned around to look at her and saw the wooden piece in her hands; with the surprised look painted on his tired face, he breathed heavily:

"Where did you get that from?"

Samantha smiled:

"It's not important where I found it, but what's important is that you please come down now.. I love it the same way I still love you, Michael."

He didn't hesitate as he came down and quickly ran to her to hold her in his shaking arms.

"I am sorry... I didn't mean to hurt you." He whispered as she placed her head on his shoulder.

They got back into their relationship and got married. Michael told Samantha that the piece of wood was meant as her birthday present, and he had wanted to give it to her that night, but instead, he buried it in that spot. He had worked on it since the first day they met even though he had never done anything like it before, but he learned it just because he knew how much Samantha loved these things.

Who drew that drawing and put it on Samantha's desk? We all know it was that angel sent from God.

As for Martin, he found himself in a hallway at the hospital. With no delay or hesitation he headed towards his ill father's room. His father hadn't woke up yet, and he began hugging him as if it's the first time they'd met, but Martin was surprised when his dad began waking up and said:

"My son.... You're here.."

Martin's happiness could not be described as he saw his dad finally wake up, and he excitingly said:

"Yes .... Yes.. I am here, and I will never leave you alone."

Yes, tears fell down from the father's eyes as he saw his son stand by him, knowing that he wasn't the best father in the most difficult times.

" I am sorry Martin... I was a bad father, but I love you son.. Please forgive me.." He uttered with eyes full of tears.

Martin smiled as he held his hand and replied:

"You don't have to apologize dad; today is a new day, and as for the past--it's gone, and you shouldn't think of it at all.

Martin's father left the hospital, and they stayed together until he married and had kids; his first born child was named after his father.

Katherine woke up only to find herself at that same alley, but she found a card sitting in front of her; when she examined it, she found out it belonged to a lawyer named Frank, and it included all of his numbers. She quickly got up and headed for a public phone and called his office, but his secretary answered, and Katherine told her that she wanted to talk to the lawyer, and she gave the secretary her name. Frank immediately took over and began:

"Are you Katherine? Jacqueline's daughter?'

Katherine didn't know how to answer, and after a long pause, she replied:

"Yes."

He got up from his desk, pulled out the chair in front of him, and continued:

"Please take a seat. I've been looking for you for a long time, but you suddenly disappeared."

She looked at him, not knowing what was going on. She was being treated like a princess; that lawyer's treatment toward her made her feel nervous and strange, but she quickly answered:

"I am sorry about that."

He looked at her: "Seems like you don't know what happened after you left the house." The lawyer took out a piece of paper from his drawer, gave it to Katherine , and ordered:

"Here.. Read this paper."

Katherine began reading it, in shock. She couldn't believe what she was reading; that tear fell from her eye suddenly. That paper was an official document, declaring Katherine's ownership of Candy World.

Her grandmother had bought the store and granted ownership to Katherine. It's the place that Katherine loved dearly, and it was a dream for her to have the store, but her grandmother made that dream come true. The most famous candy store was now hers; Mr. Frank, the lawyer, looked at her and how surprised she was:

"You know; her son came here and accused me of stealing because he thought his mother's money equaled much more than what was left. The truth is, she spent half of it buying that store for you."

From a homeless girl to the owner of the most elite candy store in the world. It's not easy to describe what Katherine was feeling, but she went to the store to stand in front it, dressed elegantly like she used to. One thing changed on the store banner; it was the name; now it read "Candy World: Jacqueline and grandmother", but the store wasn't the only thing she inherited; she also inherited the orphanage Jacqueline created. It's the place where Katherine became her daughter, and Katherine continued in her mother's footsteps. All the money she earned was spent on that orphanage.

Madison woke up finding herself at the rehabilitation center; what happened gave her the hope she didn't believe in. She was able to recover completely from her drug addiction, and she wrote a new song, composing it as well. The first place she went to was that place where the band used to meet. The sun was getting ready to depart, and its color turned to red as well as the sky's color. Madison was singing the song she had written; the words talked about her experiences, discussing the sorrow of what happened. It also expressed the meaning of friendship; these were some of the words she was singing:

I was living in heaven with trees and friends around me

I was hearing the music of birds, singing in the name of liberty

But I woke up suddenly, finding fire eating this place..

I was seeing the branches burn, and the birds crying in fear.

All my friends left me alone

All this green turned gray

I was scared and lost hope in everything

All of it was my fault

I didn't appreciate what I had

But I heard a call the sent hope within my soul

I had to express my apologies some way

So I decided to bring back life to this place

Even though the smoke was suffocating me

But I had to endure it and fix my mistakes

Madison was then surprised to hear footsteps coming closer to her. She looked, and they were the members of her band, excluding Marshall . Some were crying, while some had a sad smile; they were happy to see their leader back again; it gave them hope.

That incident wasn't missing the tears and the hugs. That place took them all back to the beautiful memories that united them in the past.

The band made a comeback and produced another album. It was a strong comeback, and people still loved Madison. That band was still in their hearts, despite everything. What proved that was that the album was the number one sold album, and it stayed on top for a few weeks.

Jessica found herself at the pond; she began looking at the water with high hopes, but the water reflected the presence of someone from behind. The vision wasn't very clear because the wind was blowing, which made a few waves in the water. She heard someone from behind saying:

"Can I set by you?"

The voice sounded familiar; Jessica was in complete disbelief. She looked behind her and almost had a meltdown when she saw--it was William.

Without a warning, she threw herself into his arms and began crying like a little kid. She pinched his face several times to make sure it wasn't a dream, but with his usual smile, he remarked:

"I am real!! I know they told you I am dead, but they also didn't know that I was alive."

Jessica was overly excited, and it's hard to explain that happiness. They both took off walking, side by side, to the farm. William stopped and looked at his dad, who sat alone in the middle of the farm, and yelled:

"Hey old man; why don't you take break from your hard work!"

William was smiling, but his voice cut through, lightning speed, to his dad's ears, who looked only to see his son standing next to Jessica. He immediately got up, and the chair fell back due to the strength of that push. He ran to William, while William also ran toward his dad. He then hugged him so tight that his bones almost broke. All of these noises were loud enough for his mother to come out and see what was going on; she saw William and began yelling in tears:

"William , my son!! You're alive!"

She was running at an insane speed toward him, which made him joke:

"Mom, you don't need to run 120 mph; 20 is enough. Either ways, you will make it here!"

He then looked to his father and continued:

"You see how fit she is while she runs; it's like she is one of the racers coming back from the Olympics!"

The atmosphere was great, and it didn't lack some tears. They weren't the tears of sadness, rather the tears of joy for the safe coming of their son, whom before this moment was counted alongside the dead.

William told them his story and what happened. He said that one time when he was on a mission, a huge explosion took place from an unknown source. Everyone was killed; some were his friends, and some were civilians because that explosion was aimed at the military base, but it killed everyone, whether they were soldiers or just normal people. William was on the ground because of that explosion, and he found an unidentified, burnt body laying next to him.

So he took off his military medal, which included his name and unit, and he put it on that body to create an illusion of his death for the people who caused the explosion. He then crept away from that place after finding everyone dead. An old woman approached him; she helped him up and too him to her home. She is not the old lady we know, but she was a real old lady who lived in that area; he continued:

"That woman took me, and I met her husband, who was sitting on a rocking chair. They knew I was from the military, but they treated me very well. The group of rebels who caused the explosion came to their house, and they hid me. I asked them why they did all of that for me, and their answer was a warm smile. The man told me that I am not their enemy, and that I am their guest, and it's their duty to serve me. They treated my wounds until I was able to move, and I went back to the base. You know what happened after that."

The soul came back to that farm after William's arrival. It became the place where you'll find the most happiness in this world. As for Jessica, she married and had kids; she lived a happy life. The man she married was Martin.

Kevin woke up, tied with ropes. He opened his eyes, knowing exactly what was happening around him, so he didn't scream or say a single word. The doctor came in and approached him:

"Kevin, how are you doing today?"

Kevin looked at him with a huge smile:

"Just fine, thank you."

The doctor felt strange, as if he was talking to a normal person:

"Are you really okay?"

Kevin smiled again while looking at the doctor:

"I know of everything I've done, and I know that Diana passed away, and I don't have a child. May I ask you something doctor?"

The doctor looked surprisingly at him:

"Yes, of course, go ahead!"

"I wan to go to my mother at the house. Please; I know I am asking for too much, but I promise, I will come back."

The doctor was looking at him, and the seriousness in Kevin's tone, so he quickly answered:

"Have it your way Kevin."

"Thank you," Kevin thanked.

The doctor then untied him, and ordered the workers to let him go. Kevin headed straight to his house, and he began searching for his mother, but he didn't find her. He went to his room to wait for her. His mother was out, but she came home. She was about to change her clothes and go to Kevin's room, as she was used to doing, but she was amazed to hear the sound of piano coming from his room. She instantly went there and found him playing the "Secret Garden" music, which he was used to playing. She was completely astonished; how can Kevin be there, and he is playing that music. That all means one thing: he escaped from the hospital. That's what she was thinking, but she was even more astounded when he stopped and said:

"Mom, you don't have to watch over me now; you can come in."

He wasn't looking at her. She came in with small steps, as if she was scared of something strange taking place, but Kevin stood up and looked at her with tears filling his eyes. He walked two steps forward and fell down to her knees, crying:

"I am sorry mother! I am sorry about everything I've done to you. You've endured my pain, and you've sacrificed so much for me, but I returned the favor by making you cry.

It's something unbelievable; from a mentally ill person, Kevin was now back with all of his normal mentality. She was happy with what she had seen and heard. She took him in with open arms, crying to see her son finally come back.

When you feel that you've lost everything , and that you're weak and scared. Just by falling into your mother's arms, you feel a strange feeling. The feeling of power and love, and that you're in the safest place on this earth.

The doctor released Kevin from the hospital because Kevin has regained his full mental abilities, despite not even being there for a full day. He went with his mother to Diana's grave and brought a new identifier to replace the one he broke. He put it down and walked closer to the grave:

"I used to tell you that you will have a boy, but now I hope it's a girl. When you have a girl, name her after my mother. I love you, and I will miss you dearly. We will meet when God calls me. Wait for me with the child until that day."

John woke up from his long coma. He felt a level of health that he had never felt before, and he found the machines all over his body, so he moved them, and he took the electrodes off his chest. Doing so, made the nurses come running with doctor because the monitor gave off a warning signal.

Both of them were amazed by John, who was standing up. What they were seeing was a miracle. A man was in a coma, and the chances of him staying alive barely reached 1%, but he now stood in front of the, as if nothing had taken place.

He notified them that he was feeling well, and he wanted to leave. The doctor told him that he must undergo some medical tests to make sure, and that it wouldn't take much time. The tests proved that John was very well. The doctor couldn't believe what those results said, so he looked at John and said:

"You're a miracle!"

John smiled, and he left the hospital. The first thing he did was to go to that abandoned building, at the mailbox to be exact. He took out those letters, and he smiled as if he was smiling at his doing. He took them and burned them while looking at the fire get bigger slowly. While he stared at those burning papers, he heard a voice from behind, calling:

"Daddy!"

His movements were suddenly paralyzed because that word had a huge effect. He turned around and saw his two daughters along with Jolie.

They both ran up to him and threw themselves into his arms. They were crying, and so was John. He couldn't believe that the two girls were in front of him, and he was hugging them. He had almost lost hope in their return, and one of them said:

"Jolie told us that you were at the hospital."

He answered:

"Yes, but thanks to God, I feel much better now. I missed you girls very much, and I never thought I'd see you again."

She went on:

"We were wrong! We didn't value what you did for us until we were separated from you. We lost the love and care that you used to give us."

The other one finished:

"We thought that if we lived with mom and her husband we would live a better life. We would go out, play, and buy whatever we wanted. Yes that happened, but no one came and read stories to us at night. We would wake up and not find covers on us, nor did we find anyone to talk to. We only knew what we've been missing after you left."

John was looking at them, and tears came down his face. He was very content, and he couldn't find the words to describe what he was feeling, so he took them in to his arms again:

" I love you.. I love you."

One of the girls looked at him and asked:

"Would there be a problem if we stayed with you forever ?"

Before she could finish, John put his finger on her mouth to stop her from talking:

"There would be a problem if you didn't! It's your home, and since you've left, I've not been able to live at that house. Bring back life to it with your arrival!"

Jolie was wiping her tears after watching that scene, but she stood still and didn't say a word. John looked at her, and the girls both said:

"We called her and asked her to bring us here. She loves you dad, and we've decided for her to be our mother."

He smiled at them both, walked toward Jolie, and asked:

"Will you marry me?"

She was overly excited, and what just asked her made her speechless, so John turned around toward the girls:

"I knew she wouldn't say yes; come one let's go."

He smiled while saying so, but Jolie didn't take notice; she finally spoke:

"John?"

He stopped, but without looking at her:

"Yes?"

She then continued:

"That night when I told you my story.. Did you hear me?"

He smiled and looked at her:

"Yes, I heard you."

The way he said so indicated that he really did hear what she said, and not just because the old lady told him. She began jumping like little kids:

"Wait for me; I am coming!!"

While walking, John turned to her:

"How did you know I was here."

She smiled:

" When I went to the hospital, they said you left. I went to the house, and I didn't find you. So I told myself that you were probably here, and I wasn't wrong."

John married Jolie, and the girls stayed with him. They left behind their real parents, whom they didn't feel any care from , yet they felt John's value when they lost him for a little while. That's why they decided to go back to their real father, who wasn't from the same flesh or blood, but he was the true father in their eyes.

Why did this happen to me?

Will you ask yourself that question?

Are you sure you'll live long enough to find the answer?

Will your whole life stop at this question?

Life is much shorter than you think, and your search for the answer is like looking for a small needle in one of the oceans; you may find that needle, but how much time will it take you to do so?

If your question changed to: what can I do while that's happening to me? Would you feel the difference?

Surely this question is much easier than hope, and you may find many answers-- all you'd have to do is choose one.

When God created us and created our brains, but he made them with limited thoughts, for no matter how intelligent a brain is, it would amount to nothing compared to his. That's because he is God, and we're humans.

If you ask the first question, no mind can answer, therefore, all you have left is the second question, and that would be answered by life, knowledge, and wisdom. Then, your heart and mind will choose the right one.

Video games.. When you decide to buy a game of that sort; you find choices for the level of difficulty. The higher the difficulty, the more determined you feel. There will come a time when you lose hope. You'll take the rest of a warrior, until you come again with more strength and will to finish that game. In the end, you succeed. You must do the same in life, for life appears much more fascinating with its difficulties.

This life is a large, humongous tree. Every tree has branches, and on top of these branches are leaves. We are those leaves. The tree get rid of the leaves that have no use to open up a space for new leaves. In both cases, we fall down from that tree, but we try to live the best moments and not let that leaf fall too fast. Make that tree lose you in sorrow and miss you.

We were all born crying, while those around us laughed in happiness to our arrival. So work hard and try until you leave this life; the others will cry, but at that moment aim to laugh while they cry. That would be the great work, and the good things you'll do. That's why you were born, so work hard to accomplish that.

The reason for what's happening to you may not be that you're a bad person, or that your fate is even worse. If you knew the reason behind the happening of all these thing, then it's great, but if not, think of this:

God remembered you; he has missed hearing your voice when you call him while praying or at any other time. He has missed your tears when you're at the most of your weakness and have no way but to return to him. The Lord is very please when he feels his greatness, and that we're all in need of him. Without him, we're worth nothing. Be proud when he remembers you, for that indicates his love for you. That's why he makes you suffer, to put you through a test. So beware of running, for when God is with you, you're not supposed to run. All you must do is have faith and patience.

If you were to choose one of these two: to be a huge building that touches the sky; one with the breathtaking scenery and most beauty, or a small building with one story; it might even be a little filthy, and not the most beautiful. If you knew that the tall building would collapse from the smallest breeze of air, while the small building will withstand any harsh weather, even a tornado or an earthquake; it will stand in it's place..

Which will you choose?